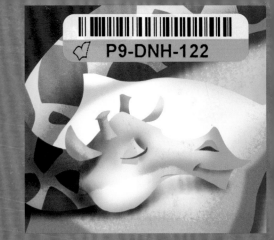

Waking Up Is Hard To Do

PERFORMED BY
Neil Sedaka

MUSIC AND LYRICS BY **Neil Sedaka**
& Howard Greenfield

CHILDREN'S LYRICS BY **Neil Sedaka**

ILLUSTRATED BY
Daniel Miyares

imagine!
Publishing
New York
www.imaginebks.com

You slept all night, now it's morning time,
That's the time to rise and shine.

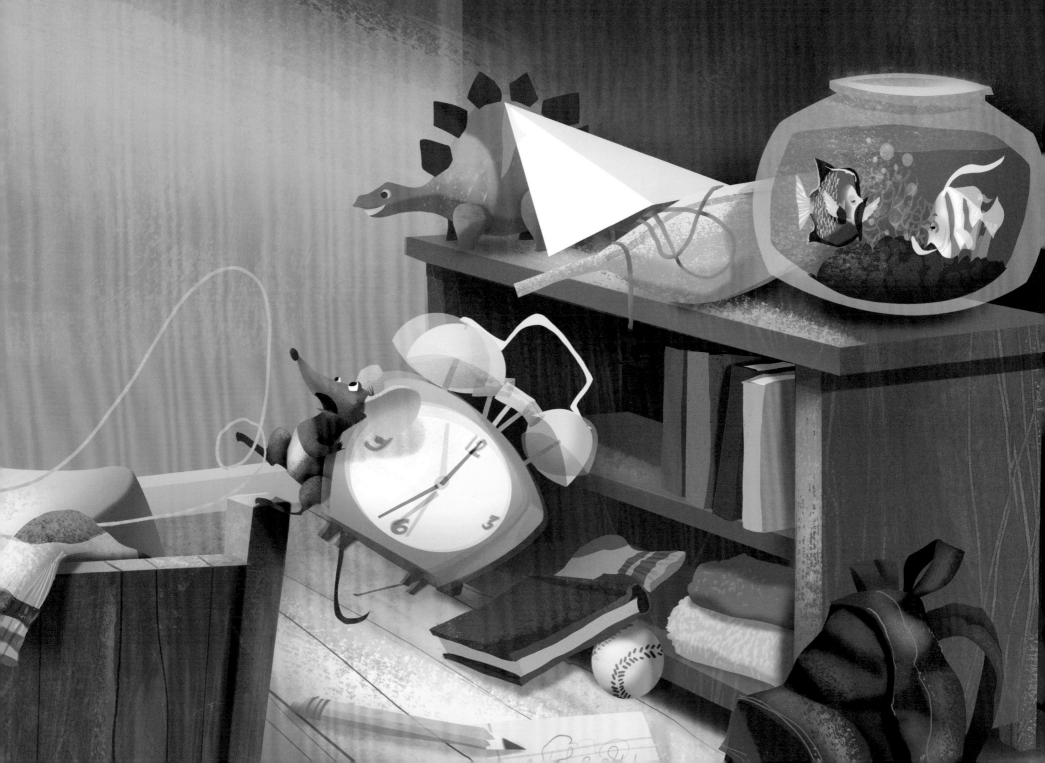

Don't you cry and don't be blue,
WAKIN' UP IS HARD TO DO.

Just brush your teeth and then get dressed.
When you comb your hair you'll look the best.

Now you know it's really true,
wakin' up is hard to do.

They say that wakin' up is hard to do.
Wear a smile, don't you be blue.

Just wipe the sleep from your eyes.
Instead of going back to bed,
You got to stretch and face the day.

Just listen to the birdies sing,

And the flowers that await the spring.

Rise and shine, your dreaming's through.

Wakin' up is hard to do.

They say that wakin' up is hard to do.
Wear a smile, don't you be blue.

Just wipe the sleep from your eyes.

Instead of going back to bed

You got to stretch and face the day.

Just listen to the birdies sing,
And the flowers that await the spring.
Rise and shine, your dreaming's through.
wakin' up is hard to do.

Down doobie doo down down, comma comma ...

Down doobie doo down down, comma comma ...

Down doobie doo down down, comma comma ...

Down doobie doo down down, comma comma ...

Dedicated to my three wonderful grandchildren, Amanda, Charlotte, & Michael Sedaka, who inspire me always. --N. S

For Lisa and Stella Jane --D. M

Performer's Note

The idea of "Waking Up Is Hard to Do" was inspired by my twin granddaughters Charlotte & Amanda (age 6), and my grandson Michael (age 4), who have grown up listening to Papa Neil's oldies. I have always found that young children related to my old songs because they are melodic, catchy, and full of hooks, so I decided to adapt my original hits to suit a new audience. The new songs did so well that when I was approached about publishing a children's book, I thought it would be a wonderful idea. I hope you enjoy the book with your children and grandchildren. Hopefully, this will be the start of many more.

Artist's Note

As a child growing up in South Carolina, I remember Neil Sedaka's songs being summer staples on the radio. I also remember singing along on many occasions, very poorly but at the top of my lungs. It is an honor to be a part of sharing that same fun and creativity with a new generation of songbirds.

Library of Congress Cataloging-in-Publication Data

Sedaka, Neil.

Waking up is hard to do / Neil Sedaka ; illustrated by Daniel Miyares.

p. cm.

Summary: An illustrated version of Sedaka's song of the same name in which an
alligator is encouraged to wake up and face the new day with a smile.

ISBN 978-1-936140-13-8 (hardcover : alk. paper)

1. Songs, English--United States--Texts. [1. Songs.] I. Miyares, Daniel, ill. II. Title.

PZ8.3.S4443Wak 2010 [E]--dc22   2010001402

10 9 8 7 6 5 4 3 2 1

Published by IMAGINE PUBLISHING, INC.
25 Whitman Road, Morganville, NJ 07751

Distributed in the United States by BookMasters Distribution Services, Inc.
30 Amberwood Parkway, Ashland, Ohio 44805

Distributed in Canada by BookMasters Distribution Services, Inc.
c /o Jacqueline Gross Associates, 165 Dufferin Street,
Toronto, Ontario, Canada M6K 3H6

Printed in China

Manufactured in May 2010
All rights reserved
Edited by Brooke Dworkin
ISBN 978-1-936140-13-8

For information about custom editions, special sales, premium and corporate purchases,
please contact Imagine Publishing, Inc. at specialsales@imaginebks.com

nething which can evolve. „

y Republic to be a home for the brave a

s has something to contribute to the life of this nation. „

o Negro problem. There is no Southern problem. There is no Northern problem. The

nt leap for mankind. „

[letting] anything happen, can stop any machine, including this machine. And it will s

at this moment, which is so important for mankind. „

vileged and humiliated. „

It's liberty or it's death. It's freedom for everybody or freedom for nob

. Turn the page. It's all a rhythm. It's all a beat. „

people. „   " We must take back our cities, and take back our culture, and take back our country. „

s we forget that we've only just begun. We're still pioneers. They, the members of the Challenger crew, were pionee

ur challenge shouldn't be anything that's just legislative. We're suppose

lution, and see the impact. „

the red hills of Georgia, the sons of former slaves a

everything. And you have certainly not lost America, for we will stand with you for as many tomorrows

ist acts. „

ica, I say: The generation before ours kept faith with us, and like them, we will pa

your own home first. And begin love there. Be

truggle for freedom than ours. „

g may be to say, 'I'm a feminist.' Because then people who love you will begin to think differently about feminism. „

nguage. That may be the measure of our lives. „

hich, with Orwellian fervor, certain accepted thoughts and speech are

tters with specific approval, after informing my superiors of the facts, as I kne

ver their own actions, they remain still part of me. „

ll. „

the future is vastly more exciting and interesting if we're a space-faring civiliz

nsible to the people they serve. „

gravity of the threat that Iraq's weapons of mass destruction pose to

Happy Valentine's Day
to one of my favorite
son-in-laws!

Love, Kris
xox

GREAT SPEECHES
That Changed the World

Publications International, Ltd.

Contributing writers: Elisabeth Andrews, Marty Strasen and Beth Taylor

Images taken from The Associated Press, Corbis, Getty Images, Library of Congress, National Archives, PIL collection, Shutterstock.com, and Wikimedia Commons

Louis Weber, CEO
Publications International, Ltd.
8140 Lehigh Avenue
Morton Grove, IL 60053

ISBN: 978-1-64030-654-7

Manufactured in China.

8 7 6 5 4 3 2 1

Table of Contents

MARIE CURIE

December 11, 1911

Polish-born French physicist Marie Curie became the first woman to win a Nobel Prize in 1903 when she shared the Prize for Physics with Henri Becquerel and her husband, Pierre Curie, for the discovery of radioactivity.

Marie Curie missed being elected the first female member of the French Academy of Sciences by two votes in 1911 to a man, but her showing was still a victory for feminism at a time when many deemed it unthinkable for a woman to be considered.

Another milestone victory followed in 1911 when Curie was the sole winner of the Nobel Prize in Chemistry. After Marie and Pierre Curie first discovered the radioactive elements polonium and radium from pitchblende in 1898, Marie continued to investigate their properties. In 1910 Marie managed to produce radium as a pure metal—shedding any doubt about the new element's existence. She also documented the properties of the radioactive elements and their compounds, leading to great breakthroughs in medicine.

In her 1911 Nobel Prize speech, Curie gave a nod to her husband and went on to relate the scientific proof of radium's existence. The scientific and medical communities celebrated both her words and her work.

Radium and New Concepts in Chemistry

" Some 15 years ago the radiation of uranium was discovered by Henri Becquerel, and two years later the study of this phenomenon was extended to other substances, first by me, and then by Pierre Curie and myself. This study rapidly led us to the discovery of new elements, the radiation of which, while being analogous with that of uranium, was far more intense. All the elements emitting such radiation I have termed *radioactive*, and the new property of matter revealed in this emission has thus received the name *radioactivity*. "

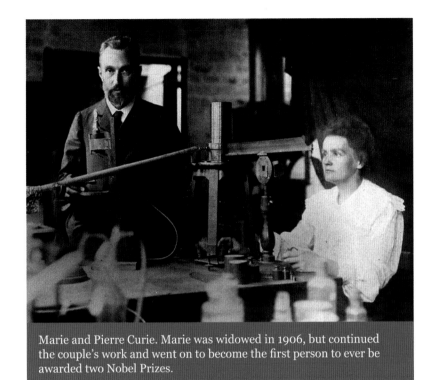

Marie and Pierre Curie. Marie was widowed in 1906, but continued the couple's work and went on to become the first person to ever be awarded two Nobel Prizes.

" We are face to face with a whole world of new phenomena belonging to a field which, despite its close connection with the fields of physics and chemistry, is particularly well-defined. In this field the importance of radium from the viewpoint of general theories has been decisive. The history of the discovery and the isolation of this substance has furnished proof of my hypothesis that *radioactivity is an atomic property of matter and can provide a means of seeking new elements*. This hypothesis has led to present-day theories of radioactivity, according to which we can predict with certainty the existence of about 30 new elements which we cannot generally either isolate or characterize by chemical methods. We also assume that these elements undergo atomic transformations, and the most direct proof in favor of this theory is provided by the experimental fact of the formation of the chemically defined element *helium* starting from the chemically defined element *radium*. "

" The task of isolating radium is the cornerstone of the edifice of the science of radioactivity. Moreover, radium remains the most useful and powerful tool in radioactivity laboratories. "

" Although radium has so far only been obtained in very small amounts, it is nevertheless true to say, in conclusion, that it is a perfectly defined and already well-studied chemical element. "

WOODROW WILSON

January 8, 1918

The "War to End All Wars" was in its final bloody year when President Woodrow Wilson spelled out a plan for peace aimed toward guiding negotiations for its end. It was an idealistic plan and one intended to dispel the notion that alliances among nations should preserve the balance of power in the world. He delivered his "Fourteen Points" before a joint meeting of Congress just days after British Prime Minister David Lloyd George listed ten points—some similar—in a speech conveying Britain's hopes as World War I approached an end.

Wilson's speech was met with mixed reactions, even among his Democratic colleagues. A translated version was delivered to the masses in Germany and Austria-Hungary, and both soldiers and citizens there saw it as a positive step toward armistice. Theodore Roosevelt and Republicans on the home front were highly critical.

Although Wilson's speech has been credited with hastening the Treaty of Versailles, which officially ended the war between Germany and the Allied Powers, that treaty was largely built with little consideration for Wilson's fourteen points. Wilson, however, did win the Nobel Peace Prize in 1919 for his efforts in restoring peace following the war.

Fourteen Points

"It will be our wish and purpose that the processes of peace, when they are begun, shall be absolutely open and that they shall involve and permit henceforth no secret understandings of any kind. The day of conquest and aggrandizement is gone by; so is also the day of secret covenants entered into in the interest of particular governments and likely at some unlooked-for moment to upset the peace of the world."

"What we demand in this war... is that the world be made fit and safe to live in; and particularly that it be made safe for every peace-loving nation which, like our own, wishes to live its own life, determine its own institutions, be assured of justice and fair dealing by the other peoples of the world as against force and selfish aggression. All the peoples of the world are in effect partners in this interest, and for our own part we see very clearly that unless justice be done to others it will not be done to us."

"I. Open covenants of peace, openly arrived at, after which there shall be no private international understandings of any kind but diplomacy shall proceed always frankly and in the public view."

"III. The removal, so far as possible, of all economic barriers and the establishment of an equality of trade conditions among all the nations consenting to the peace and associating themselves for its maintenance."

"**In regard to these essential rectifications of wrong and assertions of right we feel ourselves to be intimate partners of all the governments and peoples associated together against the Imperialists. We cannot be separated in interest or divided in purpose. We stand together until the end.**"

President Wilson addressing Congress in 1917, the year the United States entered World War I.

Birth control pioneer and advocate Margaret Sanger was scheduled to deliver her "The Morality of Birth Control" speech at the closing session of the First American Birth Control Conference on November 13, 1921, at the Town Hall in New York City. However, the police raided the meeting and arrested Sanger for disorderly conduct. Supporters from the audience followed Sanger to the police station and sang "My Country, 'Tis of Thee" in protest.

Five days later, Sanger finally delivered her "The Morality of Birth Control" address at the Park Theatre. Sanger called the incident five days earlier "a disgrace to liberty-loving people, and to all traditions we hold dear in the United States." She made the case that there was nothing immoral about birth control, particularly in a world where overpopulation had become an important issue. It was a speech that shaped the conversation in the months and years to come.

MARGARET SANGER

November 18, 1921

The Morality of Birth Control

We know that every advance that woman has made in the last half century has been made with opposition, all of which has been based upon the grounds of immorality. When women fought for higher education, it was said that this would cause her to become immoral and she would lose her place in the sanctity of the home. When women asked for the franchise, it was said that this would lower her standard of morals. "

Margaret Sanger and her sister, Ethel Byrne, on the steps of the courthouse. Both Sanger and Byrne went to trial in 1917. Both were convicted of distributing contraceptives and sentenced to 30 days in a workhouse.

" We stand on the principle that birth control should be available to every adult man and woman. We believe that every adult man and woman should be taught the responsibility and the right use of knowledge. We claim that woman should have the right over her own body and to say if she shall or if she shall not be a mother, as she sees fit. We further claim that the first right of a child is to be desired. While the second right is that it should be conceived in love, and the third, that it should have a heritage of sound health. "

" There are laws in this country which forbid the imparting of practical information to the mothers of the land. Our first step is to have the backing of the medical profession so that our laws may be changed, so that motherhood may be the function of dignity and choice, rather than one of ignorance and chance. "

" We know that the masses of people are growing wiser and are using their own minds to decide their individual conduct. The more people of this kind we have, the less immorality shall exist. For the more responsible people grow, the higher do they and shall they attain real morality. "

Sanger opened the nation's first family planning clinic in Brownsville, Brooklyn on October 16, 1916. Days later, police arrested Sanger for violating a law prohibiting the distribution of materials on contraception due to their obscene nature. The publicity surrounding Sanger's arrest, trial, and appeal brought attention to the issue.

FRANKLIN D. ROOSEVELT

March 4, 1933

America was in the painful throes of the Great Depression when Franklin D. Roosevelt defeated incumbent Herbert Hoover in the 1932 presidential election. Roosevelt promised Americans "a new deal" and won the White House in a landslide. As his inauguration approached, however, few knew how he planned to raise a largely unemployed, hungry, and despaired nation back to its feet.

In his first inaugural address, FDR confronted the nation's dilemma head-on. He blamed the greed of bankers and businessmen for America's dire predicament. Roosevelt challenged Americans to overcome the debilitating fear that had contributed to the nation's struggles. He also set the stage for the unprecedented role the federal government would play in turning around the country's fortunes. Roosevelt said he would ask Congress for "broad executive power to wage a war against the emergency," as great as the power he would be granted if we were invaded by a foreign foe.

> " The only thing we have to fear is fear itself—nameless, unreasoning, unjustified terror which paralyzes needed efforts to convert retreat into advance. In every dark hour of our national life, a leadership of frankness and of vigor has met with that understanding and support of the people themselves which is essential to victory. "

First Inaugural Address

" Only a foolish optimist can deny the dark realities of the moment. And yet our distress comes from no failure of substance. We are stricken by no plague of locusts. Compared with the perils which our forefathers conquered, because they believed and were not afraid, we have still much to be thankful for. "

" **Happiness lies not in the mere possession of money; it lies in the joy of achievement, in the thrill of creative effort. The joy, the moral stimulation of work no longer must be forgotten in the mad chase of evanescent profits.** "

Franklin D. Roosevelt's first inaugural address contained the now famous line "the only thing we have to fear is fear itself."

" Our greatest primary task is to put people to work. This is no unsolvable problem if we face it wisely and courageously. It can be accomplished in part by direct recruiting by the government itself, treating the task as we would treat the emergency of a war, but at the same time, through this employment, accomplishing greatly needed projects to stimulate and reorganize the use of our natural resources. "

" The people of the United States have not failed. In their need they have registered a mandate that they want direct, vigorous action. They have asked for discipline and direction under leadership. They have made me the present instrument of their wishes. In the spirit of the gift I take it. "

In this photograph, unemployed men wait in a soup kitchen line. When Roosevelt assumed office in 1933, unemployment had reached a staggering 25 percent. In his first inaugural address, Roosevelt stated, "Our greatest primary task is to put people to work."

WINSTON CHURCHILL

June 4, 1940

Winston Churchill became prime minister of the United Kingdom just months after the outbreak of World War II in Europe. In a series of three memorable speeches given to the House of Commons during the Battle of France, he took on the task of galvanizing the people of Great Britain for what he felt would be a long march to victory. The second of those three speeches became known as the "We Shall Fight on the Beaches" address.

Much of Churchill's "We Shall Fight on the Beaches" speech on June 4, 1940, was an account of military events. He reported the success of the Germans in overrunning the Netherlands, Belgium, and France north of the Somme, and the evacuation of British and French troops from Dunkirk. Churchill also warned the UK of possible invasion by the Nazis. Finally, he echoed a sentiment from his earlier "Blood, Toil, Tears, and Sweat" speech that, no matter how bleak a situation might seem, British forces would not relent until victory had been won.

 Our thankfulness at the escape of our Army and so many men, whose loved ones have passed through an agonizing week, must not blind us to the fact that what has happened in France and Belgium is a colossal military disaster. The French Army has been weakened, the Belgian Army has been lost, a large part of those fortified lines upon which so much faith had been reposed is gone.

We Shall Fight on the Beaches

" We shall go on to the end, we shall fight in France, we shall fight on the seas and oceans, we shall fight with growing confidence and growing strength in the air, we shall defend our Island, whatever the cost may be, we shall fight on the beaches, we shall fight on the landing grounds, we shall fight in the fields and in the streets, we shall fight in the hills; we shall never surrender. "

" **I have, myself, full confidence that if all do their duty, if nothing is neglected, and if the best arrangements are made, as they are being made, we shall prove ourselves once again able to defend our Island home, to ride out the storm of war, and to outlive the menace of tyranny, if necessary for years, if necessary alone.** "

" We are told that Herr Hitler has a plan for invading the British Isles. This has often been thought of before. When Napoleon lay at Boulogne for a year with his flat-bottomed boats and his Grand Army, he was told by someone, "There are bitter weeds in England." There are certainly a great many more of them since the British Expeditionary Force returned. "

In his "We Shall Fight on the Beaches" speech, Churchill hailed the May 26–June 4 evacuation of more than 338,000 British and French troops from the beaches of Dunkirk as a "miracle of deliverance." But he also warned, "We must be careful not to assign to this deliverance the attributes of a victory. Wars are not won by evacuations."

MOHANDAS GANDHI

August 8, 1942

For Mohandas Gandhi's entire life, the British had ruled India. His most famous call to end that rule came during a passionate speech in Bombay (now Mumbai) in August 1942, a few years into World War II. Gandhi called for a purely "nonviolent fight for India's independence." The speech launched the "Quit India" movement, a civil disobedience movement aimed at Britain's immediate withdrawal from India.

Within hours of the speech, Gandhi and most of the Indian National Congress (who supported the movement) were imprisoned without trial. Most would remain in captivity for the rest of the war. Many organizations within India sided with the British rather than with the "Quit India" movement. Among these were the Muslim League, the princely states, the police, and many Indian business owners profiting from the war.

U.S. President Franklin D. Roosevelt tried to convince British Prime Minster Winston Churchill to give in to at least some of Gandhi's demands, but Churchill refused. Indian independence, Churchill said, would not be possible until after the war ended. While the "Quit India" movement was unsuccessful, Gandhi's speech was a milestone in the fight against British rule. India finally gained independence in 1947.

> **Ours is not a drive for power, but purely a nonviolent fight for India's independence . . . A nonviolent soldier of freedom will covet nothing for himself; he fights only for the freedom of his country.**

Mohandas "Mahatma" Gandhi in 1942, the year he launched the "Quit India" movement.

> **I believe that in the history of the world, there has not been a more genuinely democratic struggle for freedom than ours.**

> Our quarrel is not with the British people; we fight their imperialism. The proposal for the withdrawal of British power did not come out of anger. It came to enable India to play its due part at the present critical juncture.

Gandhi picked up grains of salt at the end of his salt march. To protest the British taxation on salt production, Gandhi marched 241 miles to the coastal village Dandi and made illegal salt himself. Media coverage of the march drew worldwide attention to the Indian independence movement.

After studying law in London, Gandhi (center) moved to colonial South Africa in 1893. The racism he experienced there led him to his civil rights work, which focused on the racial persecution of Indians in South Africa. Gandhi returned to India in 1915 and joined the Indian National Congress.

> Every one of you should, from this moment onwards, consider yourself a free man or woman, and acts as if you are free and are no longer under the heel of this imperialism.

> Here is a mantra, a short one, that I give you. You may imprint it on your hearts and let every breath of yours give expression to it. The mantra is: 'Do or Die.' We shall either free India or die in the attempt; we shall not live to see the perpetuation of our slavery.

J. ROBERT OPPENHEIMER

November 16, 1945

Months after an American B-29 bomber dropped the first atomic bomb on August 6, 1945, the man hailed by many as the "father" of that weapon delivered a pointed speech calling them "evil." J. Robert Oppenheimer, a physics professor at the University of California–Berkeley, was selected to head the Los Alamos Laboratory during World War II. He was a key leader of the Manhattan Project, which developed the atomic weapons the United States used to devastate the Japanese cities of Hiroshima and Nagasaki. The atomic bombs killed more than 100,000 people, the majority of whom were civilians. Japan announced its surrender to the Allies on August 15, six days after the Nagasaki bombing.

In an address to the American Philosophical Society in November 1945, Oppenheimer emphasized the need for ethical application when it came to these "evil" weapons. He expressed his hope that one would never again be deployed, and his grave concern about the future of a world that now held such destructive force.

J. Robert Oppenheimer, wartime head of the Los Alamos Laboratory, is sometimes called the "father of the atomic bomb" for his role in the Manhattan Project.

 We have made a thing, a most terrible weapon, that has altered abruptly and profoundly the nature of the world. We have made a thing that, by all standards of the world we grew up in, is an evil thing.

Address to the American Philosophical Society

> " During our lifetime, perhaps atomic weapons could be either a greater or small trouble. They cannot be a small hope; they can be a great one. Sometimes, when men speak of the great hope and the great promise of the field of atomic energy, they speak not of peace, but of atomic power and of nuclear radiations. "

The Trinity test in New Mexico was the first detonation of a nuclear weapon. It was conducted on July 16, 1945, as part of the Manhattan Project. The U.S. detonated nuclear weapons over the Japanese cities of Hiroshima and Nagasaki the next month.

> " The pattern of the use of atomic weapons was set at Hiroshima. They are weapons of aggression, of surprise, and of terror. If they are ever used again, it may well be by the thousands, or perhaps by the tens of thousands. "

> " It is a practical thing to recognize as a common responsibility, wholly incapable of unilateral solution, the completely common peril that atomic weapons constitutes for the world. To recognize that only by community of responsibility is there any hope of meeting that peril. "

> " It does seem to me, necessary to explore somewhat the impact of the advent of atomic weapons on our fellow men, and the courses that might lie open for averting the disaster they invite. I think there is only one such course, and that in it lies the hope of all our futures. "

J. Robert Oppenheimer (left) and Major General Leslie Groves (right) at the Trinity test site in September 1945.

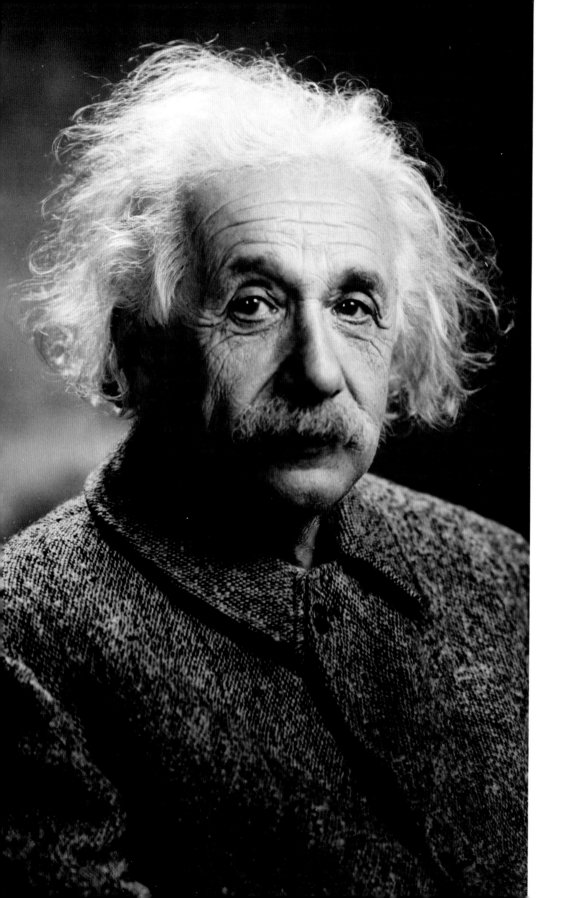

ALBERT EINSTEIN

December 10, 1945

Albert Einstein did not work on the atomic bomb, but in 1939 the world-renowned physicist had signed a letter to President Franklin D. Roosevelt urging him to accelerate nuclear research because Germans might win the "race" to build an atomic bomb. In a speech at the Fifth Nobel Anniversary Dinner just four months after the U.S. dropped atomic bombs on the Japanese cities of Hiroshima and Nagasaki, Einstein discussed the implications of such "progress." Einstein compared the contemporary physicists who produced the atomic bomb to Alfred Nobel, the Nobel Prize founder who invented dynamite.

Troubled by what he had seen since the end of World War II, Einstein, who received the Nobel Prize for Physics in 1921, called for a move toward peace. "The war is won," he said, "but the peace is not." Einstein also discussed the tragic fate of his own Jewish people during World War II, lauding the "heroic efforts" of some of the smaller countries that protected Jews from Nazis while condemning those around the world who looked on passively.

The War Is Won, the Peace Is Not

"The Nobel Anniversary celebration takes on a special significance this year. Well after our deadly struggle of many years, we are at peace again; or what we are supposed to consider as peace. And it bears a still more significant significance for the physicists who, in one way or another, were connected with the construction of the use of the atomic bomb."

"Today, the physicists who participated in forging the most formidable and dangerous weapon of all times are harassed by an equal feeling of responsibility, not to say guilt. We cannot desist from warning, and warning again, we cannot and should not slacken in our efforts to make the nations of the world, and especially their governments, aware of the unspeakable disaster they are certain to provoke unless they change their attitude toward each other and toward the task of shaping the future."

"The war is won, but the peace is not. The great powers, united in fighting, are now divided over the peace settlements. The world was promised freedom from fear, but in fact fear has increased tremendously since the termination of the war. The world was promised freedom from want, but large parts of the world are faced with starvation while others are living in abundance."

"The situation calls for a courageous effort, for a radical change in our whole attitude in the entire political concept. May the spirit that prompted Alfred Nobel to create this great institution—the spirit of trust and confidence, of generosity and brotherhood among men, prevail in the minds of those upon whose decisions our destiny rests. Otherwise, human civilization will be doomed."

Albert Einstein and J. Robert Oppenheimer at the Institute for Advanced Study, in Princeton, New Jersey. While Einstein didn't work on the atomic bomb as Oppenheimer did, the 1939 letter he signed to President Roosevelt helped spur the U.S. to engage in its own serious nuclear weapons research.

Jawaharlal Nehru's "Tryst with Destiny" speech came just hours before the clock struck midnight and signaled India's long-awaited independence from Great Britain. Speaking to the Constituent Assembly of India in New Delhi, Nehru called India's independence a triumph, but also the beginning of an opportunity that would bring additional triumphs. Nehru laid out his vision to build "a prosperous, democratic, and progressive nation."

Nehru emerged as an important leader in India's independence movement under Mohandas Gandhi's tutelage. Nehru became president of the Indian National Congress (Congress Party) in 1928 and presided over the historic 1929 session that proclaimed complete independence from the British as India's political goal.

On August 15, 1947, hours after his "Tryst with Destiny" speech, Nehru became the first prime minister of independent India. He served until his death in 1964. Throughout his years as prime minister, Nehru worked to achieve a democratic, socialist, and secular India. Nehru carried India into the modern age of scientific discovery and technological development.

JAWAHAR-LAL NEHRU

August 14, 1947

> Long years ago we made a tryst with destiny, and now the time comes when we shall redeem our pledge … At the stroke of the midnight hour, when the world sleeps, India will awake to life and freedom. A moment comes, which comes but rarely in history, when we step out from the old to the new, when an age ends, and when the soul of a nation, long suppressed, finds utterance. It is fitting that at this solemn moment we take the pledge of dedication to the service of India and her people and to the still larger cause of humanity.

Tryst with Destiny

Nehru and Gandhi in 1942. In his speech Nehru said that Gandhi "held aloft the torch of freedom." Nehru promised to "never allow that torch of freedom to be blown out, however high the wind or stormy the tempest."

"The achievement we celebrate today is but a step, an opening of opportunity, to the greater triumphs and achievements that await us. Are we brave enough and wise enough to grasp this opportunity and accept the challenge of the future?"

"The appointed day has come—the day appointed by destiny—and India stands forth again, after long slumber and struggle, awake, vital, free, and independent. The past clings on to us still in some measure and we have to do much before we redeem the pledges we have so often taken. Yet the turning point is past, and history begins anew for us.

"There is no resting for any one of us until we redeem our pledge in full, until we make all the people of India what destiny intended them to be. We are citizens of a great country, on the verge of bold advance, and we have to live up to that high standard."

Nehru signing the Constitution.

GEORGE MARSHALL

June 5, 1947

When Secretary of State George C. Marshall gave a commencement address at Harvard University on June 5, 1947, few listeners at the time realized the significance of the speech. Marshall, who had been invited to receive an honorary degree, described Europe's continued economic devastation following World War II. Marshall outlined an ambitious plan to help rebuild the continent and restore its "normal economic health." Without American support, Marshall feared that the economic crisis would lead to political chaos, destroy democratic rule, and encourage the growth of Soviet-backed communist parties across Western Europe.

Marshall's speech marked a significant change in American foreign policy, turning from isolationism to international engagement. Over the next few years, the United States delivered billions of dollars in aid to more than a dozen participating European nations through the Marshall Plan, officially known as the European Recovery Program. The Marshall Plan helped rebuild economies, promoted peace and stability in Western Europe, and prevented the spread of communism. George Marshall's role as architect of the Marshall Plan earned him the Nobel Peace Prize in 1953.

Before becoming U.S. Secretary of State, George C. Marshall was a five-star general who served as Chief of Staff of the United States Army during World War II. He later served as Secretary of Defense and President of the Red Cross.

The Marshall Plan

> " The truth of the matter is that Europe's requirements for the next three or four years of foreign food and other essential products—principally from America—are so much greater than her present ability to pay that she must have substantial additional help, or face economic, social, and political deterioration of a very grave character. "

Parade honoring the delivery of the Marshall Plan's millionth ton of food for Greece.

Tractors and other farm equipment financed with funds from the Marshall Plan arriving in France.

> " It is logical that the United States should do whatever it is able to do to assist in the return of normal economic health in the world, without which there can be no political stability and no assured peace. Our policy is directed not against any country or doctrine but against hunger, poverty, desperation, and chaos. Its purpose should be the revival of a working economy in the world so as to permit the emergence of political and social conditions in which free institutions can exist. "

> " An essential part of any successful action on the part of the United States is an understanding on the part of the people of America of the character of the problem and the remedies to be applied. Political passion and prejudice should have no part. With foresight, and a willingness on the part of our people to face up to the vast responsibility which history has clearly placed upon our country, the difficulties I have outlined can and will be overcome. "

WILLIAM FAULKNER

December 10, 1950

William Faulkner was awarded the 1949 Nobel Prize for Literature on the basis of "his powerful and artistically unique contribution to the modern American novel." The honor was bestowed the following December in Stockholm, Sweden. Faulkner delivered his speech accepting the Nobel Prize at a time of heightened atomic anxiety, when the possibility of nuclear war threatened to end humanity.

Faulkner used the platform to speak to young writers. Faulkner stated it was the duty of serious writers to put aside their fear and focus on love, sacrifice, compassion, and the human spirit. The role of the writer in this new era, Faulkner said, was to inspire humanity and help people see beyond the talk of impending destruction. Writers, he contended, could help mankind "endure and prevail"—concepts he wove throughout his short but impactful Nobel banquet speech at Stockholm City Hall in December 1950.

Faulkner was not well known before receiving the 1949 Nobel Prize for Literature. Some of his notable works include *The Sound and the Fury*, *As I Lay Dying*, *Light in August*, and *Absalom, Absalom!*

The Writer's Duty

" I feel that this award was not made to me as a man, but to my work—a life's work in the agony and sweat of the human spirit, not for glory and least of all for profit, but to create out of the materials of the human spirit something which did not exist before. So this award is only mine in trust. "

" **Our tragedy today is a general and universal physical fear so long sustained by now that we can even bear it. There are no longer problems of the spirit. There is only the question: When will I be blown up?** "

This commemorative stamp honoring William Faulkner was issued in 1987. The Nobel Prize laureate died in 1962.

" I decline to accept the end of man. It is easy enough to say that man is immortal simply because he will endure: that when the last dingdong of doom has clanged and faded from the last worthless rock hanging tideless in the last red and dying evening, that even then there will still be one more sound: that of his puny inexhaustible voice, still talking. "

" I believe that man will not merely endure: he will prevail. He is immortal, not because he alone among creatures has an inexhaustible voice, but because he has a soul, a spirit capable of compassion and sacrifice and endurance. "

" The poet's, the writer's, duty is to write about these things. It is his privilege to help man endure by lifting his heart, by reminding him of the courage and honor and hope and pride and compassion and pity and sacrifice which have been the glory of his past. The poet's voice need not merely be the record of man, it can be one of the props, the pillars to help him endure and prevail. "

Rowan Oak in Oxford, Mississippi, the home of William Faulkner. Here he wrote *A Fable*, for which he won both the Pulitzer Prize and National Book Award in 1954.

In his farewell address to the United States, President Dwight D. Eisenhower warned of the unchecked influence of the "military-industrial complex" on national policy. His speech popularized the term, which refers collectively to the nation's military forces, the private companies that produce military weapons and supplies, and the elected officials who represent districts involved in military manufacturing. He worried that the more powerful these groups became, the more political influence they would have, leading to decisions that encouraged greater military expenditures.

Eisenhower was reacting to the changes in defense spending that had occurred during the Cold War. This long-running conflict with the Soviet Union never resulted in direct combat. Instead, each side relied on ever-increasing stockpiles of weapons to deter the enemy from striking. Never before had the country committed such resources to the military in peacetime. With no end to the Cold War in sight, it appeared that weapons manufacturing would become a permanent part of the national economy.

DWIGHT D. EISENHOWER

January 17, 1961

> " We now stand ten years past the midpoint of a century that has witnessed four major wars among great nations … Despite these holocausts, America is today the strongest, the most influential, and most productive nation in the world. Understandably proud of this pre-eminence, we yet realize that America's leadership and prestige depend, not merely upon our unmatched material progress, riches, and military strength, but on how we use our power in the interests of world peace and human betterment. "

The Military-Industrial Complex

> " This conjunction of an immense military establishment and a large arms industry is new in the American experience. The total influence—economic, political, even spiritual—is felt in every city, every statehouse, every office of the federal government. We recognize the imperative need for this development. Yet we must not fail to comprehend its grave implications. Our toil, resources, and livelihood are all involved. So is the very structure of our society. "

> " **In the councils of government, we must guard against the acquisition of unwarranted influence, whether sought or unsought, by the military-industrial complex. The potential for the disastrous rise of misplaced power exists and will persist.** "

Eisenhower is shown in his role as Supreme Allied Commander in World War II, speaking to soldiers on D-Day, June 6, 1944.

> " Only an alert and knowledgeable citizenry can compel the proper meshing of huge industrial and military machinery of defense with our peaceful methods and goals, so that security and liberty may prosper together. "

Many countries celebrate May 1st as Labor Day or International Workers' Day. May Day parades such as this one in Red Square allowed the Soviet Union to display its military might. In 1958, the year this picture was taken, Eisenhower proclaimed the day "Loyalty Day" in the United States.

JOHN F. KENNEDY

January 20, 1961

As the youngest person to ever be elected president, the 43-year-old John F. Kennedy seemed to embody the claim in his inaugural address that "the torch has been passed to a new generation of Americans." For many people, his election symbolized a new era of optimism in which the country would lead global efforts to end poverty and oppression.

One of Kennedy's greatest obstacles to winning the presidency was his religion. Voters worried that, as a Roman Catholic, he would be more accountable to the pope than to the American people. However, his election seemed to indicate that Americans were ready for the inclusive "New Frontier" his campaign promised. His win, however, was by less than two thousandths of a percent. Despite his lofty rhetoric, the country remained deeply divided, with Republicans in the U.S. Congress resisting his efforts to expand federal programs for education, health care, and urban affairs. He also faced foreign policy challenges like a disastrous failed invasion of Cuba, a nuclear standoff with the Soviet Union, and the escalation of the conflict in Vietnam.

Inaugural Address

Let the word go forth from this time and place, to friend and foe alike, that the torch has been passed to a new generation of Americans—born in this century, tempered by war, disciplined by a hard and bitter peace, proud of our ancient heritage, and unwilling to witness or permit the slow undoing of those human rights to which this nation has always been committed, and to which we are committed today at home and around the world.

In your hands, my fellow citizens, more than mine, will rest the final success or failure of our course. Since this country was founded, each generation of Americans has been summoned to give testimony to its national loyalty. The graves of young Americans who answered the call to service surround the globe.

Although his assassination in 1963 cut short his presidency, Kennedy did achieve some of the goals alluded to in his inaugural address. His brief administration saw the development of the Peace Corps, the launching of the Apollo space program, and the drafting of a new civil rights bill that was passed shortly after his death.

Now the trumpet summons us again—not as a call to bear arms, though arms we need—not as a call to battle, though embattled we are—but a call to bear the burden of a long twilight struggle, year in and year out, rejoicing in hope; patient in tribulation, a struggle against the common enemies of man: tyranny, poverty, disease, and war itself.

Can we forge against these enemies a grand and global alliance, North and South, East and West, that can assure a more fruitful life for all mankind? Will you join in that historic effort?

And so, my fellow Americans, ask not what your country can do for you; ask what you can do for your country. My fellow citizens of the world, ask not what America will do for you, but what together we can do for the freedom of man.

NEWTON MINOW

May 9, 1961

Speaking to the National Association of Broadcasters in May 1961, Federal Communications Council (FCC) Chairman Newton Minow told television executives to improve the educational and social value of their programming or risk losing the license to broadcast.

At the time of Minow's speech, only three major networks existed. The percentage of households with television sets had grown during the 1950s from 9 percent to almost 90 percent. The predominant formats on television were Westerns, sitcoms, and game shows, with news and educational programming claiming only a small share of airtime.

The Federal Communications Commission was charged with ensuring that public airwaves were used for the "public interest, convenience, and necessity." Minow accused broadcasters of failing to fulfill this obligation by concerning themselves only with ratings and not with "the service of the people and the cause of freedom."

Executives took notice, introducing more nonfiction and public affairs programming. They also used dramas to address relevant social issues like poverty and health care. By the end of the decade, educational programming had taken a major leap forward, with the number of educational stations quadrupling and the newly formed Public Broadcasting Service featuring groundbreaking children's shows like *Sesame Street*.

Television and the Public Interest

" Your industry possesses the most powerful voice in America. It has an inescapable duty to make that voice ring with intelligence and with leadership. In a few years, this exciting industry has grown from a novelty to an instrument of overwhelming impact on the American people. It should be making ready for the kind of leadership that newspapers and magazines assumed years ago, to make our people aware of their world. "

" Just as history will decide whether the leaders of today's world employed the atom to destroy the world or rebuild it for mankind's benefit, so will history decide whether today's broadcasters employed their powerful voice to enrich the people or to debase them. "

In 1950, when this photograph was taken, there were only 96 TV stations in the United States. By 1970, there were close to 700. During his tenure as FCC chair, Minow saw through the passage of a 1962 act that mandated that all television sets carry UHF as well as VHF channels, which resulted in an expansion of the number of stations throughout the country.

Minow served two years as chair of the FCC. In later life, he served on the Board of Governors at PBS and wrote several books on television and broadcasting.

" I invite each of you to sit down in front of your television set when your station goes on the air and stay there, for a day, without a book, without a magazine, without a newspaper, without a profit and loss sheet or a rating book to distract you. Keep your eyes glued to that set until the station signs off. I can assure you that what you will observe is a vast wasteland. "

" You must provide a wider range of choices, more diversity, more alternatives. It is not enough to cater to the nation's whims; you must also serve the nation's needs. And I would add this: that if some of you persist in a relentless search for the highest rating and the lowest common denominator, you may very well lose your audience. "

King's speech, the last of the day, followed speeches by other civil rights leaders and performances by musicians such as Mahalia Jackson, Bob Dylan, and Joan Baez.

Martin Luther King, Jr.'s "I Have a Dream" speech contributed to the passage of the Civil Rights Act of 1964 that outlawed discrimination based on race, color, religion, or national origin.

Born in Atlanta, Georgia, King was a Baptist minister and one of the most influential figures in the civil rights movement. As the head of the Southern Christian Leadership Conference, he dedicated himself to nonviolent resistance as a means of protesting racial inequality. Known as a powerful speaker, King helped bring national attention to desegregation efforts like sit-ins and the Montgomery Bus Boycott. He was arrested several times for his participation in civil rights demonstrations, but gained support from Presidents John F. Kennedy and Lyndon B. Johnson.

In 1963, along with several other leaders, King organized a "March on Washington" to support the pending civil rights legislation that would later become the Civil Rights Act. During the event, he delivered his speech to an interracial crowd of more than 200,000 people gathered at the Lincoln Memorial in Washington, D.C.

MARTIN LUTHER KING, JR.

August 28, 1963

> " Now is the time to rise from the dark and desolate valley of segregation to the sunlit path of racial justice. Now is the time to lift our nation from the quicksands of racial injustice to the solid rock of brotherhood. Now is the time to make justice a reality for all of God's children. "

I Have a Dream

> Even though we face the difficulties of today and tomorrow, I still have a dream. It is a dream deeply rooted in the American dream. I have a dream that one day this nation will rise up and live out the true meaning of its creed: "We hold these truths to be self-evident, that all men are created equal."

> **I have a dream that one day on the red hills of Georgia, the sons of former slaves and the sons of former slave owners will be able to sit down together at the table of brotherhood.**

> I have a dream that one day even the state of Mississippi, a state sweltering with the heat of injustice, sweltering with the heat of oppression, will be transformed into an oasis of freedom and justice.

> **I have a dream that my four little children will one day live in a nation where they will not be judged by the color of their skin but by the content of their character.**

> When we allow freedom ring, when we let it ring from every village and every hamlet, from every state and every city, we will be able to speed up that day when *all* of God's children, black men and white men, Jews and Gentiles, Protestants and Catholics, will be able to join hands and sing in the words of the old Negro spiritual: *Free at last! Free at last! Thank God Almighty, we are free at last!*

Despite fears of violence and disorder, the protesters assembled peacefully. *The New York Times* called it "the greatest assembly for a redress of grievances that this capital has ever seen."

Malcolm X at a rally in Harlem in June 1963.

MALCOLM X

April 12, 1964

During the peak of the American civil rights movement in the 1960s, prominent African American leader Malcolm X offered an alternative to the integration-based approach of Dr. Martin Luther King, Jr. He advocated instead for black nationalism, a philosophy that centered on giving African Americans political and economic control of their communities.

Born Malcolm Little, he dropped his last name after joining the Nation of Islam, a religious organization that combined Muslim teachings with black nationalist ideals. Changing or dropping surnames was a custom among the organization's followers because many African American surnames originated with slave owners.

In 1964, Malcolm split from the Nation of Islam due to conflicts with the group's leader, Elijah Muhammad. Shortly after, Malcolm delivered one of his most famous speeches, "The Ballot or the Bullet," in Detroit, Michigan. In it he compared the plight of blacks in America to that of Africans who were then in the process of decolonization. He explained that white colonialists had exploited both groups. The solution, he said, was not to request civil rights from an oppressive government but to reclaim ownership of their civic life through any means necessary.

Members of the Nation of Islam assassinated Malcolm X the following year.

The Ballot or the Bullet

 We suffer political oppression, economic exploitation, and social degradation, all of them from the same enemy. The government has failed us; you can't deny that. Any time you're living in the 20th century, 1964, and you're walking around here singing, "We Shall Overcome," the government has failed you. This is part of what's wrong with you. You do too much singing. Today it's time to stop singing and start swinging.

Black nationalism is a self-help philosophy ... This is a philosophy that eliminates the necessity for division and argument, because if you're black, you should be thinking black. And if you're black and you're not thinking black at this late date, well, I'm sorry for you.

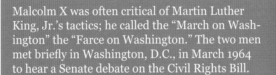
Malcolm X was often critical of Martin Luther King, Jr.'s tactics; he called the "March on Washington" the "Farce on Washington." The two men met briefly in Washington, D.C., in March 1964 to hear a Senate debate on the Civil Rights Bill.

 Every nation on the African continent that has gotten its independence brought it about through the philosophy of nationalism. And it will take black nationalism to bring about the freedom of 22 million Afro-Americans, here in this country, where we have suffered colonialism for the past 400 years.

I say it's the ballot or the bullet. It's liberty or it's death. It's freedom for everybody or freedom for nobody.

You don't have a revolution in which you love your enemy. And you don't have a revolution in which you are begging the system of exploitation to integrate you into it. Revolutions overturn systems. Revolutions destroy systems.

Malcolm X's widow, Betty Shabazz, is found to the right in this photograph from his graveside. More than 14,000 mourners attended a public viewing before Malcolm X's funeral service. Actor Ossie Davis, delivering the eulogy, called Malcolm a "stormy, controversial and bold young captain," and "our own black shining prince."

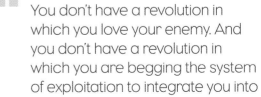

BARRY GOLDWATER

July 16, 1964

Goldwater delivered his acceptance speech on the final day of the Republican National Convention, after he won his party's nomination decisively on the first ballot.

Known as "Mr. Conservative," Arizona Senator Barry Goldwater helped usher in a new era of right-wing Republicanism with his successful bid for the Republican presidential nomination in 1964. Although he lost the election to incumbent President Lyndon B. Johnson, the rhetoric of Goldwater's campaign decisively split the conservative faction of the party from its more liberal Eastern bloc, paving the way for Ronald Reagan to win the presidency in 1980.

Goldwater pushed for reducing the size and power of the federal government in nearly all areas except defense. He maintained that the communist threat necessitated a massive military buildup. His anti-communist stance was so extreme that he once joked about the nuclear bomb, "Let's lob one into the men's room at the Kremlin."

This tendency to speak off the cuff—he also told a panel of news reporters, "sometimes I think this country would be better off if we could just saw off the Eastern Seaboard and let it float out to sea"—contributed to Goldwater's election defeat. His opponents were able to paint him as an aggressive, impulsive reactionary who could lead the country into nuclear war.

> **The good Lord raised this mighty Republic to be a home for the brave and to flourish as the land of the free—not to stagnate in the swampland of collectivism, not to cringe before the bully of communism.**

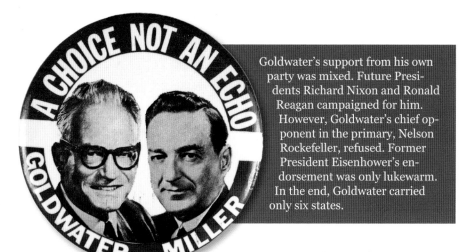

Goldwater's support from his own party was mixed. Future Presidents Richard Nixon and Ronald Reagan campaigned for him. However, Goldwater's chief opponent in the primary, Nelson Rockefeller, refused. Former President Eisenhower's endorsement was only lukewarm. In the end, Goldwater carried only six states.

" The Republican cause demands that we brand communism as a principal disturber of peace in the world today. Indeed, we should brand it as the only significant disturber of the peace, and we must make clear that until its goals of conquest are absolutely renounced and its rejections with all nations tempered, communism and the governments it now controls are enemies of every man on Earth who is or wants to be free. "

" Let our Republicanism, so focused and so dedicated, not be made fuzzy and futile by unthinking and stupid labels. I would remind you that extremism in the defense of liberty is no vice. And let me remind you also that moderation in the pursuit of justice is no virtue. "

" It is our cause to dispel the foggy thinking which avoids hard decisions in the illusion that a world of conflict will somehow mysteriously resolve itself into a world of harmony, if we just don't rock the boat or irritate the forces of aggression—and this is hogwash.

" It is further the cause of Republicanism to remind ourselves, and the world, that only the strong can remain free, that only the strong can keep the peace. "

The young women who donned cowboy hats as they campaigned for Goldwater were dubbed "Goldwater Girls." They included a young Hillary Clinton in their number.

MARIO SAVIO

December 2, 1964

Mario Savio was one of the student leaders at the University of California at Berkeley who organized massive demonstrations to protest the school's restrictions on political activity on campus. Over several months beginning in September 1964, the students held a series of rallies and sit-ins that persuaded the university to ease its restrictions and also sparked the larger student protest movement of the 1960s.

The Berkeley student protests became known as the Free Speech Movement. Initially, student political groups resisted the administration's rules by setting up tables to offer political literature in prohibited areas. The situation escalated when eight participants were suspended and, soon after, one was arrested by campus police. Student supporters quickly surrounded the police car, resulting in a standoff that lasted more than 32 hours.

Savio's speech preceded a sit-in during which some 1,000 protesters occupied the university's administration building, Sproul Hall. More than 600 policemen were dispatched and more than 800 people were arrested. The following day, a crowd of 5,000 rallied in support of the students' cause.

The administration ultimately capitulated. Berkeley and many other university campuses soon became major sites of political activity, especially for protests against the Vietnam War.

The steps of Sproul Hall where Mario Savio delivered his speech are now called the "Mario Savio Steps." Savio served several months in prison in 1967 for his role in the sit-in. His activism brought him to the attention of the FBI, which monitored him for many years.

> There's a time when the operation of the machine becomes so odious, makes you so sick at heart that you can't take part. You can't even passively take part. And you've got to put your bodies upon the gears and upon the wheels, upon the levers, upon all the apparatus, and you've got to make it stop. And you've got to indicate to the people who run it, to the people who own it, that unless you're free the machine will be prevented from working at all!

Sit-in Address on the Steps of Sproul Hall

> **One thousand people sitting down some place, not letting anybody by, not [letting] anything happen, can stop any machine, including this machine. And it will stop!**

> Sometimes, the form of the law is such as to render impossible its effective violation as a method to have it repealed. Sometimes, the grievances of people are more—extend more—to more than just the law, extend to a whole mode of arbitrary power, a whole mode of arbitrary exercise of arbitrary power.

Flyers such as the one to the right were circulated in order to organize protests. Organizers wrote, "We demand the same rights as citizens on campus, as we or any citizen is guaranteed off campus," and "The administration will have to amend the United States Constitution before they can take away our rights."

Mon Nov 9

NOON TODAY, WE SHALL RESUME THE EXERCIZE OF OUR RIGHTS!

THE ADMINISTRATION WILL HAVE TO AMEND THE UNITED STATES CONSTITUTION BEFORE THEY CAN TAKE AWAY OUR RIGHTS.

SINCE OCTOBER 2, WE HAVE VOLUNTARILY ABDICATED MANY OF OUR RIGHTS IN A HOPE OF WORKING OUT A REASONABLE SETTLEMENT WITH THE ADMINISTRATION.

THERE HAVE BEEN NO SIGNS OF PROGRESS.

WE HEREBY LIFT THE SELF-IMPOSED MORATORIUM ON OUR CIVIL LIBERTIES.

WE MUST ACT

WE MUST ALL JOIN TOGETHER TO PROTECT OUR CIVIL LIBERTIES AND THE CONSTITUTION.

COME

NOON TODAY IN FRONT OF SPROUL HALL (if it's not raining. Otherwise come to the eaves between the Student Union and the Dining Commons.)

WE DEMAND THE SAME RIGHTS AS CITIZENS ON CAMPUS, AS WE OR ANY CITIZEN IS GUARANTEED OFF CAMPUS.

Free Speech Movement   (labor donated)

Singer Joan Baez, center, came to lend support to the sit-in.

> We're going to have classes on [the] First and Fourteenth Amendments. We're going to spend our time learning about the things this university is afraid that we know. We're going to learn about freedom up there, and we're going to learn by doing.

LYNDON B. JOHNSON

March 15, 1965

Adopting the refrain of civil rights activists, "We Shall Overcome," President Lyndon B. Johnson urged the U.S. Congress to pass a voting rights bill that would end the widespread disenfranchisement of African Americans. The proposal, which became the Voting Rights Act of 1965, prohibited discriminatory practices such as literacy tests and poll taxes, and ensured federal oversight of elections. Although existing laws nominally guaranteed equal voting rights for all citizens, African Americans attempting to exercise these rights in the South commonly encountered a variety of hostile tactics.

Johnson's speech came one week after the "Bloody Sunday" march in Selma, Alabama, in which hundreds of civil rights demonstrators were attacked by police using nightsticks and tear gas. Media coverage of that event, along with the killing of a white minister and activist during the protests that followed, helped to mobilize public support for the Voting Rights Act.

We Shall Overcome

> **There is no Negro problem. There is no Southern problem. There is no Northern problem. There is only an American problem.**

> And we are met here tonight as Americans—not as Democrats or Republicans; we're met here as Americans to solve that problem. This was the first nation in the history of the world to be founded with a purpose.

> The great phrases of that purpose still sound in every American heart, North and South: "All men are created equal." "Government by consent of the governed." "Give me liberty or give me death." And those are not just clever words, and those are not just empty theories. In their name Americans have fought and died for two centuries and tonight around the world they stand there as guardians of our liberty risking their lives. Those words are promised to every citizen that he shall share in the dignity of man. This dignity cannot be found in a man's possessions. It cannot be found in his power or in his position. It really rests on his right to be treated as a man equal in opportunity to all others. It says that he shall share in freedom. He shall choose his leaders, educate his children, provide for his family according to his ability and his merits as a human being.

> This bill will establish a simple, uniform standard which cannot be used, however ingenious the effort, to flout our Constitution. It will provide for citizens to be registered by officials of the United States Government, if the state officials refuse to register them. It will eliminate tedious, unnecessary lawsuits which delay the right to vote. Finally, this legislation will insure that properly registered individuals are not prohibited from voting.

Johnson signed the Voting Rights Act into law on August 6, 1965.

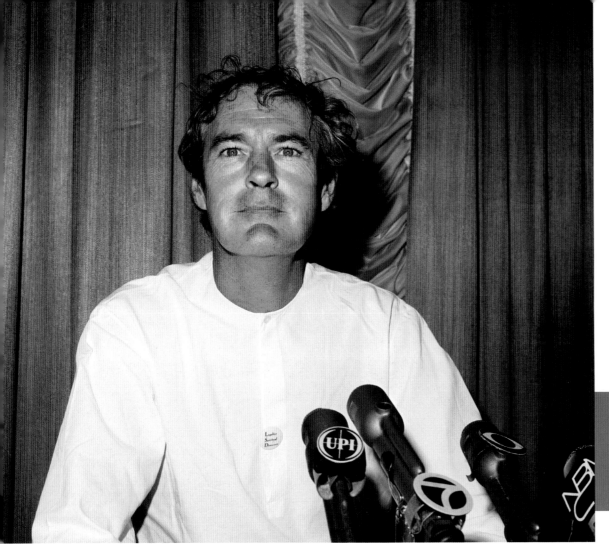

TIMOTHY LEARY

September 19, 1966

Timothy Leary used the phrase "turn on, tune in, and drop out" at the 1966 press conference in New York where he announced the formation of a new religion, the League of Spiritual Discovery. Leary argued that the use of hallucinogenic drugs was central to the practice of this religion, and therefore protected by the Constitution. Only a few weeks later, LSD was made illegal in the United States.

The "turn on, tune in, drop out" catchphrase of 1960s counterculture came from psychologist Timothy Leary. Along with his close friend Richard Alpert (later known as Ram Dass), he helped inspire the hippie generation to abandon traditional social mores in favor of spiritual exploration and personal expression.

Leary coined the phrase shortly after he and Alpert were dismissed from the faculty at Harvard University, where they had been conducting controversial experiments that involved giving graduate students the hallucinatory drug psilocybin. Their interest in incorporating LSD into their research, coupled with the revelation that some undergraduates had access to their

drugs, proved too much for university officials. Both psilocybin and LSD were, however, legal at the time.

Leary went on to become a popular speaker and icon of the counterculture movement. He brought the phrase "turn on, tune in, drop out" to prominence at San Francisco's 1967 Human Be-In, a gathering of some 20,000 people in Golden Gate Park. The event focused on themes like communal living, ecological awareness, and a rejection of consumerism. The Be-In helped anoint San Francisco as the center of the emerging hippie culture. The movement continued to flourish there during that year's "Summer of Love."

Turn On, Tune In, and Drop Out

> **Turn on, tune in, and drop out. Period. End of paragraph. Turn the page. It's all a rhythm. It's all a beat.**

Many people flocked to the Haight-Ashbury district of San Francisco during the "Summer of Love." The Mamas and The Papas, who released a song whose lyrics included the phrase, "If you're going to San Francisco, be sure to wear some flowers in your hair" immortalized the phenomenon. Government and media attention, even when disapproving, only brought more people. However, many people left the area in the fall to return to school or simply to leave behind a place that had become overcrowded.

> You have to start building a better model. Building a better building. Building a better temple. Building a better home. Building a better language. Building a better music. It's always been done that way.

> Don't get attracted by the thing you're building because you've got to drop out. And it's a cycle. Turn on, tune in, drop out. Keep it going.

Over 10,000 people attended Carmichael's speech at Berkeley, California. Carmichael also used the opportunity to speak strongly against the war in Vietnam and the draft.

Black nationalist Stokely Carmichael began his involvement with civil rights as a student at Howard University. There he joined the Student Nonviolent Coordinating Committee (SNCC), an organization known for its successful voter registration drives and its contribution to the sit-ins and Freedom Rides of the early 1960s.

As a result of his participation in these activities, Carmichael was arrested dozens of times and once spent 49 days in jail. He also saw protestors beaten and killed by white policemen and segregationists. Through these experiences, he became disillusioned with the idea of passive resistance, and embraced a more radical approach to civil rights activism.

Carmichael popularized the term "black power" to capture his goal of galvanizing the black community to work for its own empowerment. By the mid-1960s, he had become opposed to multiracial efforts to end discrimination. He voiced these ideas in a speech at the University of California at Berkeley in 1966, stating, "Black people must be seen in positions of power, doing and articulating for themselves."

STOKELY CARMICHAEL

October 29, 1966

> " We have been tired of trying to prove things to white people. We are tired of trying to explain to white people that we're not going to hurt them. We are concerned with getting the things we want, the things that we have to have to be able to function. The question is, "can white people allow for that in this country?" The question is, "will white people overcome their racism and allow for that to happen in this country?" If that does not happen, brothers and sisters, we have no choice but to say very clearly, "Move over, or we're going to move on over you." "

Carmichael continued to give speeches at college campuses throughout the year that followed. He broke with the SNCC in 1967. He moved to Guinea in 1969, changed his name to Kwame Ture, and spent his remaining 30 years advocating for "mass political organization on a Pan-African scale."

Opposite page: The Black Panther movement, which originated in California with Huey Newton and Bobby Seale, called for full employment, adequate housing, and equal education, as well as exemption from military service for black men and an end to police brutality directed towards black people. It set up a number of social programs in black communities, such as the Free Breakfast for Children Program. The group's outlook was militant; some members openly carried loaded weapons, allowable by California law at that time, to "police the police."

> " In order to understand white supremacy we must dismiss the fallacious notion that white people can give anybody their freedom. No man can give anybody his freedom. A man is born free. "

> " It is clear to me that we have to wage a psychological battle on the right for black people to define their own terms, define themselves as they see fit, and organize themselves as they see it. "

> " We are now engaged in a psychological struggle in this country, and that is whether or not black people will have the right to use the words they want to use without white people giving their sanction to it; and that we maintain, whether they like it or not, we're going to use the word "Black Power." "

ROBERT F. KENNEDY

April 4, 1968

Robert F. Kennedy was in Indiana campaigning for the Democratic nomination for president when he learned that civil rights leader Martin Luther King, Jr. had been assassinated in Memphis, Tennessee. The crowd that gathered to see him at his last stop in Indianapolis had not heard the news. The police chief advised him to call off the appearance, fearing a riot in the mostly African American neighborhood where Kennedy was scheduled to speak. But Kennedy stood up on the back of a flatbed truck, without any police escort, and told the crowd what had happened.

He spoke for only five minutes, imploring his listeners not to let the event be a cause for hatred or racial division. He shared a poem by the Greek playwright Aeschylus about despair bringing wisdom "through the awful grace of God."

After Kennedy left, the crowd dispersed. While there were riots in many other cities around the country, Indianapolis remained quiet that night. Kennedy went on to win five out of six of the primaries during the two months that followed. But then he, too, was fatally shot by an assassin.

At the time that Kennedy delivered his speech, little was known about the murder or the man who was eventually convicted, James Earl Ray. Kennedy did note that, "the evidence evidently is that there were white people who were responsible."

Remarks on Martin Luther King, Jr.'s Assassination

" I have some very sad news for all of you, and, I think, sad news for all of our fellow citizens, and people who love peace all over the world; and that is that Martin Luther King was shot and was killed tonight in Memphis, Tennessee. "

" Martin Luther King dedicated his life to love and to justice between fellow human beings. He died in the cause of that effort. In this difficult day, in this difficult time for the United States, it's perhaps well to ask what kind of a nation we are and what direction we want to move in. "

" What we need in the United States is not division; what we need in the United States is not hatred; what we need in the United States is not violence and lawlessness, but is love, and wisdom, and compassion toward one another; and a feeling of justice toward those who still suffer within our country, whether they be white or whether they be black. "

Dr. Martin Luther King, Jr. was in Memphis with other civil rights leaders, including Dr. Ralph Abernathy and Rev. Jesse Jackson (shown here the day after the assassination), to support striking sanitation workers.

" The vast majority of white people and the vast majority of black people in this country want to live together, want to improve the quality of our life, and want justice for all human beings that abide in our land. "

Kennedy and his wife, Ethel, met with King's widow, Coretta Scott King, to give their condolences.

Richard J. Daley delivered a welcoming speech on August 26, the first day of the convention, in which he pledged, "As long as I am mayor of this city, there's going to be law and order in Chicago."

Chicago Mayor Richard J. Daley's infamous slip of the tongue served to capture the chaos of the Democratic National Convention (DNC) in 1968. During the four-day event, anti-Vietnam War protesters filled the parks and streets of Chicago, Illinois, despite Daley's refusal to grant them permits. Police responded with such violence that a government-funded study later described their actions as a "police riot."

The convention took place during a year of extreme unrest. The assassination of Martin Luther King, Jr. led to riots across the country, the Vietnamese Tet Offensive struck a major blow against public confidence in the American war effort, and the assassination of Robert F. Kennedy left the Democratic Party without one of its leading anti-war candidates.

Daley knew that protests were likely and was determined to keep control of the city. He assembled close to 12,000 police officers, 7,500 Illinois National Guardsmen, 7,500 Army troops, and 1,000 Secret Service agents. Clashes between police and protesters started the night before the convention and continued over several days.

The bloody street scenes and the fractious, unruly convention in Chicago helped turn the political tide toward Republican presidential candidate Richard Nixon and his promise to restore "law and order."

RICHARD J. DALEY

September 9, 1968

DNC Protests in Chicago

> **The confrontation was not created by the police. The confrontation was created by the people who charged the police. Gentlemen, get the thing straight, once and for all. The policeman isn't there to create disorder. The policeman is there to preserve disorder.**

Mayor Daley, sitting with Illinois delegates at the 1968 Democratic National Convention, reacted to a nominating speech given by Senator Abraham Ribicoff in which he criticized the tactics of the Chicago police against anti-Vietnam War protesters.

Opposite page: During the most violent encounter known as the "Battle of Michigan Avenue," police beat people indiscriminately, injuring reporters and bystanders as well as protesters.

NEIL ARMSTRONG

July 20, 1969

As Neil Armstrong stepped off the ladder of the *Apollo II* lunar module and onto the moon's surface, becoming the first man to walk on the moon, he paused to acknowledge the NASA space program's tremendous accomplishment. He had prepared the statement in advance and intended to say, "one small step for a man," but the excitement of the moment caused him to omit the article unintentionally.

The *Apollo II* mission fulfilled the goal President John F. Kennedy had set eight years earlier, when he told Congress, "I believe that this nation should commit itself to achieving the goal, before this decade is out, of landing a man on the moon and returning him safely to the earth." Kennedy's ambition was to upstage the Soviet Union's space flight successes, which had included launching the *Sputnik* satellite into orbit and sending the first man into space.

Although Cold War rivalry was a major factor in expanding NASA's agenda, the two countries later pooled their resources for a number of space projects. The *International Space Station*, a multinational Earth-orbiting research facility, is one such successful collaboration.

Armstrong in the lunar module after his famous walk and speech.

The photograph shows Armstrong setting his footprint on the moon. Armstrong, the commander of the mission, was followed on the moon's surface by Edwin "Buzz" Aldrin, Jr., the pilot of the lunar module *Eagle*. The third man in the crew, Michael Collins, piloted the command module *Columbia*, which remained in orbit around the moon.

> **That's one small step for man, one giant leap for mankind.**

The *Apollo 11* astronauts were celebrated with a ticker-tape parade in New York City after their successful mission. In the back of the lead car (from left to right): Edwin "Buzz" Aldrin, Jr., Michael Collins, and Neil Armstrong.

The *Apollo 11* lunar landing mission crew (from left to right): Neil Armstrong, Michael Collins, and Edwin "Buzz" Aldrin, Jr.

Agnew, speaking to journalists in April 1973, expressed "full confidence" in Nixon on the Watergate matter.

SPIRO AGNEW

November 13, 1969

" As with other American institutions, perhaps it is time that the networks were made more responsive to the views of the nation and more responsible to the people they serve. "

In a speech delivered in Des Moines, Iowa, Vice President Spiro Agnew accused television news networks of delivering biased, incomplete coverage of world events, particularly when reporting on President Richard Nixon's administration. National opinion, he argued, was being determined by a small number of reporters whom he described as "a tiny, enclosed fraternity of privileged men, elected by no one."

Agnew, who was governor of Maryland before becoming vice president, was known for his verbally creative dismissals of his critics. He is remembered for slinging such epithets as "nattering nabobs of negativism," and "hopeless, hysterical hypochon-

driacs of history." Agnew's criticisms helped fuel an ongoing conservative attack on the mainstream media. His accusation of "liberal bias" still endures, and the growth of right-wing political media outlets may be attributed in some measure to his observations.

Despite what Agnew described as his "salutary" effect on the media, he left his office in disgrace in 1973. Accused of committing tax fraud, bribery, conspiracy, and extortion during his gubernatorial career, he eventually pleaded no contest to a single charge of tax evasion and became the second vice president in history to resign.

Television News Coverage

"Tonight I want to discuss the importance of the television medium to the American people. No nation depends more on the intelligent judgment of its citizens. And no medium has a more profound influence over public opinion. Nowhere in our system are there fewer checks on such vast power. So nowhere should there be more conscientious responsibility exercised than by the news media. The question is, "Are we demanding enough of our television news presentations?" "And are the men of this medium demanding enough of themselves?"

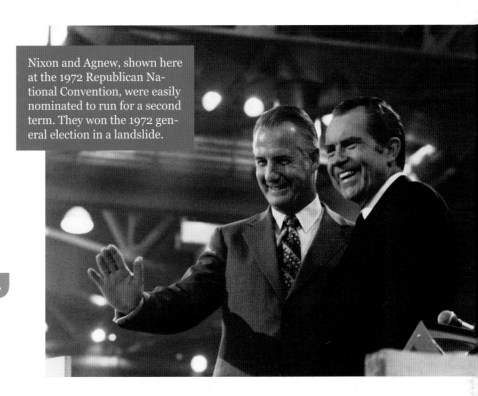

Nixon and Agnew, shown here at the 1972 Republican National Convention, were easily nominated to run for a second term. They won the 1972 general election in a landslide.

Agnew is shown here leaving court in October 1973. As a result of his plea of no contest to tax evasion, he was fined, put on probation, and disbarred in Maryland.

"I'm not asking for government censorship or any other kind of censorship. I am asking whether a form of censorship already exists when the news that 40 million Americans receive each night is determined by a handful of men responsible only to their corporate employers and is filtered through a handful of commentators who admit to their own set of biases.

A virtual monopoly of a whole medium of communication is not something that democratic people should blithely ignore.

SHIRLEY CHISHOLM

August 10, 1970

Born in Brooklyn, New York, Shirley Chisholm entered politics following a career in education. After serving in the New York State Legislature for four years, she ran for a seat in the U.S. House of Representatives. In winning the election, she became the first African American woman elected to the U.S. House of Representatives, where she served from 1969 through 1983.

Chisholm was a strong proponent of the Equal Rights Amendment to the Constitution, which would guarantee women protection from discrimination under state and federal laws. Speaking in support of the amendment in the U.S. House of Representatives, she stated that,

"Discrimination against women, solely on the basis of their sex, is so widespread that it seems to many persons normal, natural, and right." While the amendment gained approval in Congress in 1972, it was never ratified by the requisite majority of states, and so never became law.

In 1972, Shirley Chisholm announced her candidacy in the Democratic presidential primary. She was both the first black major-party candidate and the first woman to run as a Democratic presidential candidate. Although George McGovern won the nomination at the convention, Chisholm garnered votes from 152 delegates, placing her fourth in the field of 13 candidates.

Equal Rights Amendment

 House Joint Resolution 264, before us today, which provides for equality under the law for both men and women, represents one of the most clear-cut opportunities we are likely to have to declare our faith in the principles that shaped our Constitution. It provides a legal basis for attack on the most subtle, most pervasive, and most institutionalized form of prejudice that exists. Discrimination against women, solely on the basis of their sex, is so widespread that is seems to many persons normal, natural, and right.

In a speech announcing her candidacy in the Democratic presidential primary, Chisholm said, "I have faith in the American people. I believe that we are smart enough to correct our mistakes. I believe that we are intelligent enough to recognize the talent, energy, and dedication, which all Americans including women and minorities have to offer."

The argument that this amendment will not solve the problem of sex discrimination is not relevant... Of course laws will not eliminate prejudice from the hearts of human beings. But that is no reason to allow prejudice to continue to be enshrined in our laws—to perpetuate injustice through inaction.

The time is clearly now to put this House on record for the fullest expression of that equality of opportunity which our Founding Fathers professed. They professed it, but they did not assure it to their daughters, as they tried to do for their sons. The Constitution they wrote was designed to protect the rights of white, male citizens. As there were no black Founding Fathers, there were no founding mothers—a great pity, on both counts. It is not too late to complete the work they left undone.

JOHN KERRY

April 22, 1971

Years before he held political office, John Kerry addressed the Senate Foreign Relations Committee in Washington, D.C., on behalf of the Vietnam Veterans Against the War. He spared no details in delivering his message.

Kerry brought up the Winter Soldier investigation in which more than 100 Vietnam veterans testified to war crimes committed by the U.S. in Southeast Asia. Kerry described testimony in which veterans told of how they "had personally raped, cut off ears, cut off heads, taped wires from portable telephones to human genitals and turned up the power, cut off limbs, blown up bodies, randomly shot at civilians, razed villages," and other atrocities. Kerry contended that these crimes were committed on a daily basis "with the full awareness of officers at all levels of command." The administration, he said, had done veterans the "ultimate dishonor" in disowning them and the sacrifices they had made for their country.

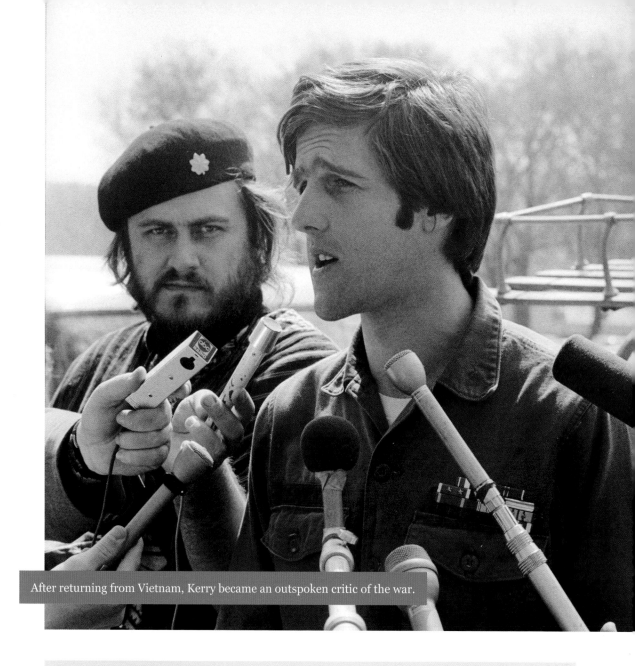

After returning from Vietnam, Kerry became an outspoken critic of the war.

> " The country doesn't know it yet but it's created a monster, a monster in the form of millions of men who have been taught to deal and to trade in violence, and who are given the chance to die for the biggest nothing in history; men who have returned with a sense of anger and a sense of betrayal which no one has yet grasped. "

Vietnam Veterans Against the War

"We are probably angriest about all that we were told about Vietnam and about the mystical war against communism. We found that not only was it a civil war, an effort by a people who had for years been seeking their liberation from any colonial influence whatsoever, but also we found that the Vietnamese... were hard put to take up the fight against the threat we were supposedly saving them from."

"We saw America lose her sense of morality as she accepted very coolly a My Lai and refused to give up the image of American soldiers that hand out chocolate bars and chewing gum."

In his address, Kerry said that the Vietnamese "only wanted to work in rice paddies without helicopters strafing them and bombs with napalm burning their villages and tearing their country apart."

"To justify the loss of one American life in Vietnam, Cambodia, or Laos by linking such loss to the preservation of freedom... is to us the height of criminal hypocrisy, and it's that kind of hypocrisy which we feel has torn this country apart."

"Our own scars and stumps of limbs are witness enough for others and for ourselves. We wish that a merciful God could wipe away our own memories of that service as easily as this administration has wiped their memories of us."

Kerry was elected to the U.S. Senate in 1985. He was the Democratic nominee in the 2004 presidential election, losing to Republican George W. Bush. Kerry served as Secretary of State in the Obama administration.

JOHN KERRY | 57

GERALD R. FORD

September 8, 1974

When Gerald Ford was sworn in as president following Richard Nixon's resignation, many people breathed a sigh of relief. After two years of investigations surrounding Nixon's alleged cover-up of the break-in to the Democratic National Committee headquarters at the Watergate hotel, Ford promised, "our long national nightmare is over." His approval ratings hit 70 percent during his first month.

But just 30 days after taking the oath of office, Ford made a decision that would cause his popularity to plummet. On a Sunday morning, he informed the nation that he was granting Richard Nixon a full pardon. He explained his feelings that Nixon could not receive a fair trial. More importantly, he argued, his decision would avoid a drawn-out trial process that would only extend the country's humiliation and anguish.

Much of the public was outraged. There were accusations of a "corrupt bargain" in which Nixon had forfeited the presidency to then-Vice President Ford in exchange for a pardon. When questioned by a member of the House of Representatives, Ford insisted, "There was no deal, period, under no circumstances." But his administration retained a stigma, if not of conspiracy, then of poor judgment.

> " There are no historic or legal precedents to which I can turn in this matter, none that precisely fit the circumstances of a private citizen who has resigned the presidency of the United States. But it is common knowledge that serious allegations and accusations hang like a sword over our former president's head. "

Address on Pardoning Richard Nixon

> We are a nation under God, so I am sworn to uphold our laws with the help of God. And I have sought such guidance and searched my own conscience with special diligence to determine the right thing for me to do with respect to my predecessor in this place, Richard Nixon, and his loyal wife and family. Theirs is an American tragedy in which we all have played a part. It could go on and on and on, or someone must write the end to it. I have concluded that only I can do that, and if I can, I must.

> My conscience tells me clearly and certainly that I cannot prolong the bad dreams that continue to reopen a chapter that is closed. My conscience tells me that only I, as president, have the constitutional power to firmly shut and seal this book. My conscience tells me it is my duty, not merely to proclaim domestic tranquility but to use every means that I have to insure it.

> I, Gerald R. Ford, president of the United States, pursuant to the pardon power conferred upon me by Article II, Section 2, of the Constitution, have granted and by these presents do grant a full, free, and absolute pardon unto Richard Nixon for all offenses against the United States which he, Richard Nixon, has committed or may have committed.

BARBARA JORDAN

July 12, 1976

In her keynote speech to the 1976 Democratic National Convention, Texas Congresswoman Barbara C. Jordan opened by reflecting on the historical peculiarity of her own presence at the podium. She noted that in the 144 years during which the party had been convening, "it would have been most unusual for any national political party to ask a Barbara Jordan to deliver a keynote address." It was obvious to those listening that she referred to her status as both the first woman and the first African American to be the convention's featured speaker.

The fact that she had been selected, she said, demonstrated the party's commitment to inclusiveness and unity. These values positioned the party to build what she described as a "national community," forged through civic participation.

> **"** We are a people in search of a national community. We are a people trying not only to solve the problems of the present, unemployment, inflation, but we are attempting on a larger scale to fulfill the promise of America. We are attempting to fulfill our national purpose, to create and sustain a society in which all of us are equal. **"**

Barbara Jordan delivering her keynote address on July 12, 1976.

" This is the great danger America faces—that we will cease to be one nation and become instead a collection of interest groups: city against suburb, region against region, individual against individual; each seeking to satisfy private wants. If that happens, who then will speak for America? Who then will speak for the common good? "

Right: Jordan's speech set a cohesive tone after the disorganization and mayhem of the 1968 and 1972 conventions. In the wake of Richard Nixon's resignation, that appearance of stability helped secure the presidency for Democratic candidate Jimmy Carter.

" **A spirit of harmony will survive in America only if each of us remembers that we share a common destiny; if each of us remembers, when self-interest and bitterness seem to prevail, that we share a common destiny.** "

The 1976 Democratic National Convention was held in New York City's Madison Square Garden.

" A nation is formed by the willingness of each of us to share in the responsibility for upholding the common good. A government is invigorated when each one of us is willing to participate in shaping the future of this nation. In this election year, we must define the "common good" and begin again to shape a common future. "

Egyptian President Anwar Sadat addressed the Israeli parliament, the Knesset, in Arabic. Israeli Prime Minister Menachem Begin responded in Hebrew.

ANWAR SADAT

November 20, 1977

When Egyptian President Anwar Sadat stood to speak to the Israeli parliament, his presence in Jerusalem was in itself astonishing. Since Israel's formation in 1948, Egypt had joined other Arab countries in denouncing the Jewish nation, refusing to so much as recognize its statehood. Territorial disputes had led to four wars between the two countries in the previous three decades.

The most recent war in 1973 had been at Sadat's own instigation. His forces, backed by Syria and aided by the Soviet Union, attacked Israel on the Jewish holy day of Yom Kippur. Although the conflict ended in a ceasefire negotiated by the United Nations, Egypt's early successes demonstrated more military might than it had exhibited in previous Arab-Israeli conflicts.

Yet Sadat had come to Jerusalem to seek a lasting peace. "Any life that is lost in war is a human life, be it that of an Arab or an Israeli," he told the assembly. He called repeatedly for "a permanent peace based on justice," in which all Arab and Israeli people could live securely within their borders.

The speech was a breakthrough in the peace process. With the aid of American President Jimmy Carter, the two countries soon signed a peace treaty. Sadat and Israeli Prime Minister Menachem Begin were awarded the Nobel Peace Prize for their achievement.

Peace Based on Justice

In 1978, Sadat, Begin, and Carter spent twelve days at Camp David in Maryland hammering out a set of agreements called the Camp David Accords. A formal peace treaty was signed at the White House on March 26, 1979. In this picture from that day, Sadat is shown to Carter's left and Begin to his right.

" I have come to you so that together we might build a durable peace based on justice to avoid the shedding of one single drop of blood by both sides. It is for this reason that I have proclaimed my readiness to go to the farthest corner of the earth. "

" Today I tell you, and declare it to the whole world, that we accept to live with you in permanent peace based on justice. We do not want to encircle you or be encircled ourselves by destructive missiles ready for launching, nor by the shells of grudges and hatred. "

" **How can we achieve a durable peace based on justice? In my opinion, and I declare it to the whole world from this forum, the answer is neither difficult nor impossible, despite long years of feud, blood vengeance, spite and hatred, and breeding generations on concepts of total rift and deep-rooted animosity. The answer is not difficult, nor is it impossible.** "

Soldiers in the Yom Kippur War.

JIMMY E. CARTER

July 15, 1979

Carter delivered his "Crisis of Confidence" speech exactly three years after he accepted his party's nomination for the presidency.

In June 1979, President Jimmy Carter returned from a Tokyo economic summit to find that the nation's energy problems had hit a crisis point. With gas prices continuing to skyrocket and shortages causing long lines at the pumps, Americans had lost patience with the federal government's inability to improve the situation. Carter's approval ratings had fallen to 25 percent.

Unsure how to proceed, Carter retreated to Camp David and called in a stream of advisers that included, in his words, "business and labor, teachers and preachers, governors, mayors, and private citizens." For ten days he listened to their assessments of his presidency and the nation's predicament.

Then, in a televised address, Carter stated, "The true problems of our nation are much deeper, deeper than gasoline lines or energy shortages, deeper even than inflation or recession." Citing a "crisis of confidence" in both government and the American dream, he called for a national commitment to unity and self-sacrifice.

> " I want to speak to you first tonight about a subject even more serious than energy or inflation. I want to talk to you right now about a fundamental threat to American democracy. "

Crisis of Confidence

> The threat is nearly invisible in ordinary ways. It is a crisis of confidence. It is a crisis that strikes at the very heart and soul and spirit of our national will. We can see this crisis in the growing doubt about the meaning of our own lives and in the loss of a unity of purpose for our nation.

> Little by little we can and we must rebuild our confidence. We can spend until we empty our treasuries, and we may summon all the wonders of science. But we can succeed only if we tap our greatest resources—America's people, America's values, and America's confidence.

Some states instituted odd-even rationing in an attempt to shorten lines at the pumps. The days that drivers could buy gas were determined by whether their license plate ended in an odd or even number.

> We simply must have faith in each other, faith in our ability to govern ourselves, and faith in the future of this nation. Restoring that faith and that confidence to America is now the most important task we face.

Carter attended an economic summit in Tokyo in June 1979 where the U.S. and several other industrialized nations agreed to set limits on the amount of oil they would import and consume.

Thatcher is shown leaving 10 Downing Street, the seat of government headquarters and the prime minister's official residence, after a meeting on April 2 about the Falkland Islands.

MARGARET THATCHER

April 3, 1982

British Prime Minister Margaret Thatcher was both the first woman to lead a major Western democracy and the longest-serving prime minister of the United Kingdom during the 20th century. Her tenure would likely have been cut short, however, were it not for the Falklands War in 1982.

The Falkland Islands, which lie off the coast of Argentina, had been under British control since 1833. However, Argentina had long attempted to claim sovereignty over the islands. In 1982, an Argentine military junta seized the islands by force. Thatcher addressed the House of Commons on April 3, the day after the invasion, asserting that the territory would remain in British hands. Her successful defense of the Falklands ensured her own reelection, while the defeated junta was replaced by civilian rule.

Prior to the Falklands campaign, Thatcher's political career was in jeopardy. She took office as prime minister in 1979 in the midst of severe economic decline. Initially, Thatcher's efforts to roll back socialist policies and privatize the manufacturing industry led to massive unemployment and rising inflation. Protecting the Falklands boosted her popularity enough to win a second term.

Invasion of the Falkland Islands

 For the first time for many years, British sovereign territory has been invaded by a foreign power. After several days of rising tension in our relations with Argentina, that country's armed forces attacked the Falkland Islands yesterday and established military control of the islands.

The ten-week Falklands conflict ended when Argentina surrendered on June 14, 1982, returning the islands to British control. In all, 650 Argentine military personnel, 255 British military personnel, and three Falkland Islanders were killed in the war.

I must tell the House that the Falkland Islands and their dependencies remain British territory. No aggression and no invasion can alter that simple fact. It is the Government's objective to see that the islands are freed from occupation and are returned to British administration at the earliest possible moment.

The people of the Falkland Islands, like the people of the United Kingdom, are an island race. Their way of life is British; their allegiance is to the Crown. They are few in number, but they have the right to live in peace, to choose their own way of life and to determine their own allegiance.

 We cannot allow the democratic rights of the islanders to be denied by the territorial ambitions of Argentina.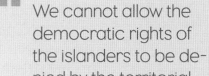

Like U.S. President Ronald Reagan, Thatcher was dedicated to a conservative political philosophy that opposed government participation in the economy. Thatcher's political recovery after the Falklands campaign allowed her to enact sweeping reforms, from widespread economic privatization and deregulation to strict controls on union organizing.

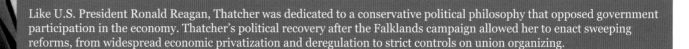

GERALDINE FERRARO

July 19, 1984

New York Congresswoman Geraldine Ferraro became the first woman to appear on a major party national ticket when Democratic presidential candidate Walter Mondale selected her as his running mate in 1984. In her acceptance speech at the Democratic National Convention, Ferraro outlined the Democratic platform's key planks. She talked about ensuring equal opportunity for all, preserving Social Security, and stopping the nuclear arms race.

Ferraro had a strong congressional record of advocating for women, older adults, and the environment. Prior to her three terms in the House of Representatives, she was an assistant district attorney in Queens, where she helped create a Special Victims Bureau to handle cases of domestic violence and rape.

Her selection initially energized voters. Media attention, however, soon turned to Ferraro's husband's finances. Ferraro was reluctant to reveal the details of her husband's real estate holdings for fear it would hurt his business. Her hesitation spurred negative headlines. She eventually submitted their tax returns for public scrutiny, which showed that many rumors were unfounded. But by then the issue had already dominated much of the campaign season. With the strong economy favoring incumbent President Ronald Reagan, Mondale and Ferraro lost in a landslide.

Ferraro giving her speech at the Democratic National Convention.

VP Nomination Acceptance Address

> " Tonight, the daughter of a woman whose highest goal was a future for her children talks to our nation's oldest party about a future for us all. Tonight, the daughter of working Americans tells all Americans that the future is within our reach, if we're willing to reach for it. Tonight, the daughter of an immigrant from Italy has been chosen to run for [vice] president in the new land my father came to love. "

Mondale announced his choice of Ferraro as his running mate on July 12. In a speech on that day, Ferraro highlighted her ties to the working class and noted that Mondale's choice said, "a lot about him, about where the country has come, and about where we want to lead it."

> " Our faith that we can shape a better future is what the American dream is all about. The promise of our country is that the rules are fair. If you work hard and play by the rules, you can earn your share of America's blessings. "

> " To all the children of America, I say: The generation before ours kept faith with us, and like them, we will pass on to you a stronger, more just America. "

> " By choosing a woman to run for our nation's second highest office, you send a powerful signal to all Americans: There are no doors we cannot unlock. We will place no limits on achievement. If we can do this, we can do anything. "

A button from the 1984 campaign.

NOW! 1984

Chavez speaking to workers at a 1985 rally against pesticides.

> " All my life, I have been driven by one dream, one goal, one vision: to overthrow a farm labor system in this nation that treats farm workers as if they were not important human beings. Farm workers are not agricultural implements; they are not beasts of burden to be used and discarded. "

CESAR CHAVEZ

November 9, 1984

Arizona native Cesar Chavez was ten years old when his family lost their farm in the Great Depression. He spent the rest of his youth traveling across the Southwest as his family searched for employment as migrant farm workers. Chavez quit school after the eighth grade to work full-time in the fields.

Chavez witnessed the extreme poverty and exploitation of many migrant workers, and racism directed against Latinos. In 1962, after a decade spent working for civil rights and worker's rights, he founded the labor union that became the United Farm Workers of America (UFW). In the decades that followed, he spearheaded a number of political organizing efforts that relied on nonviolent tactics such as strikes, boycotts, and fasts.

In a 1984 speech to the Commonwealth Club in San Francisco, California, Chavez spoke of the history of the UFW and the enduring need for it. "Thousands of farm workers live under savage conditions, beneath trees and amid garbage," he said. "Vicious rats gnaw at them as they sleep."

But Chavez believed in future progress. He pointed to the role of the UFW in raising political awareness among the Latino population and predicted that Latinos would grow in numbers and political power.

Commonwealth Club Address

"How could we progress as a people even if we lived in the cities, while the farm workers, men and women of our color, were condemned to a life without pride? How could we progress as a people while the farm workers, who symbolized our history in this land, were denied self-respect? How could our people believe that their children could become lawyers and doctors and judges and business people while this shame, this injustice, was permitted to continue?"

Chavez went on a 25-day hunger strike in early 1968 to protest violence against striking workers. He is shown here during that time at a rally attended by Robert F. Kennedy.

"The UFW was the beginning. We attacked that historical source of shame and infamy that our people in this country lived with. We attacked that injustice, not by complaining, not by seeking handouts, not by becoming soldiers in the war on poverty; we organized."

The United Farm Workers of America (UFW) supported successful strikes and boycotts of grapes and lettuce.

"Once social change begins it cannot be reversed. You cannot uneducate the person who has learned to read. You cannot humiliate the person who feels pride. You cannot oppress the people who are not afraid anymore."

RONALD W. REAGAN

January 28, 1986

Reagan delivering his speech on the evening of the explosion.

On January 28, 1986, millions of people tuned in to watch the space shuttle *Challenger* take off from Florida's Kennedy Space Center. Unknown to the crew or flight engineers, the cold weather that morning had compromised the material holding together the rocket boosters that launched the shuttle into space. Seconds after liftoff, a leak near the motor of one of the rockets caused the *Challenger* to explode over the Atlantic Ocean.

The disaster killed all seven people onboard, including New Hampshire schoolteacher Christa McAuliffe. She was to be the first private citizen in space and was scheduled to give two in-orbit lessons that would be simulcast to students around the country. Due to this "Teacher in Space Project," thousands of schoolchildren saw the *Challenger* explode.

President Ronald Reagan was scheduled to give the State of the Union address that evening, but postponed it so he could speak about the tragedy. Although he later commissioned an investigation into the cause of the accident, his speech that evening praised everyone involved with the mission.

> **We've grown used to the idea of space, and, perhaps we forget that we've only just begun. We're still pioneers. They, the members of the *Challenger* crew, were pioneers.**

Space Shuttle Challenger Tragedy

Ronald Reagan with his aides, watching a replay of the disaster. On January 31, Reagan delivered another speech at a memorial service. He said, "We will always remember them, these skilled professionals, scientists and adventurers, these artists and teachers and family men and women, and we will cherish each of their stories."

" We'll continue our quest in space. There will be more shuttle flights and more shuttle crews and, yes, more volunteers, more civilians, more teachers in space. Nothing ends here; our hopes and our journeys continue. "

The *Challenger* crew. Front row: Michael J. Smith, Francis R. Scobee, Ronald McNair. Back row: Ellison Onizuka, Christa McAuliffe, Gregory Jarvis, Judith Resnik.

" The future doesn't belong to the fainthearted; it belongs to the brave. The *Challenger* crew was pulling us into the future, and we'll continue to follow them. "

" The crew of the space shuttle *Challenger* honored us by the manner in which they lived their lives. We will never forget them, nor the last time we saw them, this morning, as they prepared for their journey and waved goodbye. "

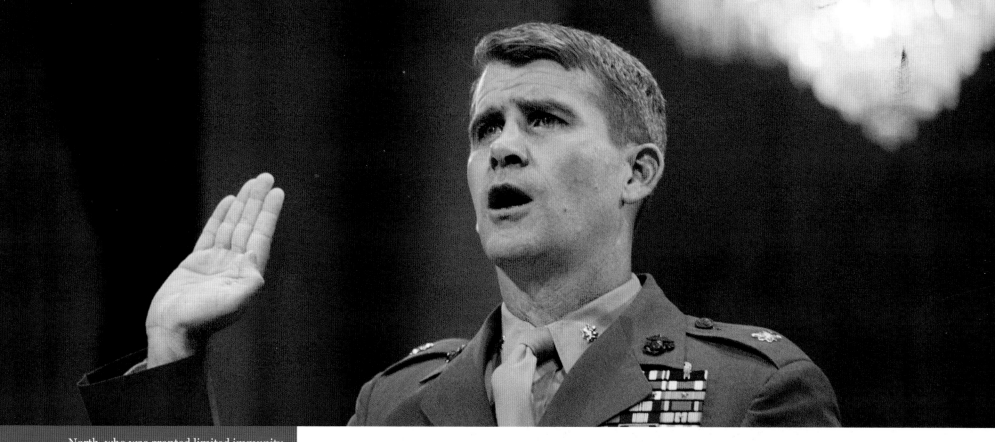

OLIVER NORTH

July 8, 1987

Oliver North, the deputy director of political-military affairs for the National Security Council during the early 1980s, coordinated many of the illegal activities that collectively came to be known as the Iran-Contra affair. He was directly involved in providing support to the revolutionary contras in Nicaragua, selling arms to Iran, and diverting proceeds from those sales to the contras.

Assistance to the contras violated the Boland Amendment that specifically prohibited the U.S. from backing the group's military efforts against the socialist government of Nicaragua. The weapons sales, intended to persuade Iran to release U.S. hostages held in Lebanon, violated an embargo and President Ronald Reagan's campaign promise never to negotiate with terrorists. The diversion of funds from one covert operation to the other added another layer of secrecy and illegality.

It was never clear exactly where these decisions were made along the chain of command. Reagan had instructed his National Security Adviser Robert McFarlane with respect to the contras, "Do whatever you have to do to help these people keep body and soul together." He also approved the arms sales. He denied any knowledge of a connection between the two.

Iran-Contra Testimony

> "As I told you yesterday, I was going to tell you the truth—the good, the bad, and the ugly. Well, this is the truth. I did probably the grossest misjudgment that I've made in my life. I then tried to paper over that whole thing by sending two phony documents back to Mr. Robinette. It was not an exercise in good judgment. I don't believe I have any particular monopoly on bad judgment."

> "Insofar as I can recall, I always acted on major matters with specific approval, after informing my superiors of the facts, as I knew them, the risks, and the potential benefits."

> "The contras, the Nicaraguan freedom fighters, are people—living, breathing, young men and women—who have had to suffer a desperate struggle for liberty, with sporadic and confusing support from the United States of America. Armies need food and consistent help. They need a flow of money, of arms, clothing, and medical supplies."

> "I was authorized to do everything that I did"
> —Oliver North

> "It is the Congress which must accept at least some of the blame in the Nicaraguan freedom fighters matter. Plain and simple, the Congress is to blame because of the fickle, vacillating, unpredictable, on-again-off-again policy toward the Nicaraguan democratic resistance, the so-called "contras.""

President Reagan received the Tower Commission Report about the Iran-Contra affair from John Tower (left) and Edmund Muskie (right) on February 26, 1987. In a March 1987 address Reagan acknowledged his administration's responsibility even as he denied personal knowledge: "A few months ago I told the American people I did not trade arms for hostages. My heart and my best intentions still tell me that's true, but the facts and the evidence tell me it is not."

ANN RICHARDS

July 18, 1988

In her straightforward, down-home Southern style, Texas state treasurer Ann Richards charmed the crowd at the 1988 Democratic National Convention in Atlanta, Georgia. Only the second woman in history to serve as the convention's keynote speaker, Richards delivered an uplifting address filled with memorable quips and jabs at Republican presidential nominee George H. W. Bush.

Despite Richards's criticism, Bush went on to beat Democratic candidate Michael Dukakis in that year's election. Two years later, Richards became the governor of Texas with a surprising win against wealthy rancher Clayton Williams. The political sparring between Richards and the Bush family, however, was far from over. In 1994, Governor Richards sought reelection against the elder Bush's son, George W. Bush. She underestimated her opponent, ran a lackluster campaign, and lost the election. This victory paved the way for George W. Bush to move directly from the governor's mansion to the White House.

In her address, Richards insisted, "We want answers and their answer is that 'something is wrong with you.' Well nothing's wrong with you. Nothing's wrong with you that you can't fix in November!"

> " Under this administration we have devoted our resources into making this country a military colossus. But we've let our economic lines of defense fall into disrepair. The debt of this nation is greater than it has ever been in our history. We fought a world war on less debt than the Republicans have built up in the last eight years. You know, it's kind of like that brother-in-law who drives a flashy new car, but he's always borrowing money from you to make the payments. "

1988 DNC Keynote Address

> **Ginger Rogers did everything that Fred Astaire did. She just did it backwards and in high heels.**

> **Poor George. He can't help it. He was born with a silver foot in his mouth.**

> This election is a contest between those who are satisfied with what they have and those who know we can do better ... It's about the American dream—those who want to keep it for the few and those who know it must be nurtured and passed along.

> We believe that America is still a country where there is more to life than just a constant struggle for money. And we believe that America must have leaders who show us that our struggles amount to something and contribute to something larger—leaders who want us to be all that we can be.

Richards debating George W. Bush during the 1994 Texas gubernatorial race.

VÁCLAV HAVEL

January 1, 1990

Playwright Václav Havel endured years of political persecution before being elected Czechoslovakia's last president following the nonviolent Velvet Revolution. Over six weeks in late 1989, the Velvet Revolution (also called the Gentle Revolution) peacefully toppled Czechoslovakia's communist government, leading to the country's first democratic elections in more than 40 years, and eventually the birth of two independent states—the Czech Republic and Slovakia.

Havel was elected interim president of Czechoslovakia on December 29, 1989, and was reelected to the presidency in July 1990. Following the division of Czechoslovakia in 1993, Havel was elected president of the new Czech Republic.

Havel spoke frankly in his address to the nation on New Year's Day 1990. He noted that his predecessors had falsely claimed that Czechoslovakia was flourishing and said, "I assume you did not propose me for this position so that I, too, would lie to you." Instead, Havel described the sad state of the country's economy, education system, and environment. He challenged citizens to participate in moving the country in a positive direction.

Václav Havel in 2010. Havel served as the Czech Republic's first president (1993–2003).

New Year's Address

" Our country is not flourishing... Entire branches of industry are producing goods that are of no interest to anyone, while we are lacking the things we need. A state which calls itself a workers' state humiliates and exploits workers. Our obsolete economy is wasting the little energy we have available... We have polluted the soil, rivers, and forests bequeathed to us by our ancestors, and we have today the most contaminated environment in Europe. "

Demonstrators in Prague during the 1989 Velvet Revolution.

" The worst thing is that we live in a contaminated moral environment. We fell morally ill because we became used to saying something different from what we thought. We learned not to believe in anything, to ignore one another, to care only about ourselves. Concepts such as love, friendship, compassion, humility, or forgiveness lost their depth and dimension. "

" **Freedom and democracy include participation and therefore responsibility from us all.** "

" We had all become used to the totalitarian system and accepted it as an unalterable fact of life, and thus we helped to perpetuate it. In other words, we are all—though naturally to differing extents—responsible for the operation of totalitarian machinery. None of us is just its victim; we are all its co-creators. "

" I dream of a republic independent, free, and democratic, of a republic economically prosperous and yet socially just; in short, a humane republic which serves the individual and which therefore holds the hope that the individual will serve it in turn. "

NELSON MANDELA

February 11, 1990

After 27 years as a political prisoner, South African anti-apartheid activist Nelson Mandela was freed on February 11, 1990. A crowd of 50,000 people welcomed him at Cape Town City Hall, where he stood on the balcony to speak.

"I greet you all in the name of peace, democracy, and freedom for all," he told listeners. The statement held great meaning for a country so long entrenched in racial discrimination and disenfranchisement, violent uprisings, and civilian slaughter at the hands of police and military forces. The establishment of apartheid in 1948 had created a legal system under which the white minority systematically denied political rights to black Africans and those of other races. Many protesters had been jailed like Mandela or killed during anti-apartheid uprisings.

By the 1980s international pressure had mounted against the South African government. The domestic resistance movement gained momentum, even as Prime Minister William Botha attempted to appease critics by repealing some aspects of apartheid. When F. W. de Klerk succeeded Botha in 1989, he recognized the need to move toward a fully inclusive democracy. One of de Klerk's first acts was to release Mandela. The two men worked together to draft a new constitution and institute universal suffrage. In 1994, Mandela became president of South Africa.

Mandela upon his release from prison.

Freedom For All

> "I greet you all in the name of peace, democracy, and freedom for all. I stand here before you not as a prophet but as a humble servant of you, the people."

> "Today the majority of South Africans, black and white, recognize that apartheid has no future. It has to be ended by our own decisive mass action in order to build peace and security. The mass campaigns of defiance and other actions of our organizations and people can only culminate in the establishment of democracy."

Mandela with F. W. de Klerk in 1994. After Mandela became president, he appointed F. W. de Klerk as his deputy president. The two men shared the Nobel Peace Prize in 1993.

> "The future of our country can only be determined by a body which is democratically elected on a non-racial basis. Negotiations on the dismantling of apartheid will have to address the overwhelming demands of our people for a democratic, non-racial, and unitary South Africa. There must be an end to white monopoly on political power and a fundamental restructuring of our political and economic systems to ensure that the inequalities of apartheid are addressed and our society thoroughly democratized."

> "The sight of freedom looming on the horizon should encourage us to redouble our efforts. It is only through disciplined mass action that our victory can be assured. We call on our white compatriots to join us in the shaping of a new South Africa. The freedom movement is a political home for you too."

> "Our march to freedom is irreversible. We must not allow fear to stand in our way. Universal suffrage on a common voters' role in a united democratic and non-racial South Africa is the only way to peace and racial harmony."

FIDEL CASTRO

September 28, 1990

Castro at a rally in Havana in 1990.

> **History will record the honor, dignity, and courage that Cuba acted with at this moment, which is so important for mankind.**

Revolutionary leader Fidel Castro took control of Cuba in 1959 after his 800 guerrilla fighters defeated the 30,000-man army of dictator Fulgencio Batista. Castro set up the first communist government in the Western Hemisphere, thereby alienating the United States and securing political partnership with the Soviet Union.

To a degree Castro's government achieved his goals of providing a high level of education, health care, and employment to all Cuban citizens. These privileges, however, came at the cost of both political freedom and economic growth.

In a 1990 speech that marked the 30th anniversary of the establishment of the Committees for the Defense of the Revolu-

tion, Castro celebrated the revolution but noted the economic effects that unrest in Eastern Europe and the Soviet Union were having on Cuba. He asserted that the Soviet Union had made "great efforts to meet its commitments to our country." But he also acknowledged that future trade was uncertain. He called on people to maintain their support for the revolution and work for Cuba's complete economic independence. "Save the Cuban Revolution," he said. "Save socialism in Cuba."

The collapse of the Soviet Union in 1991, and the loss of its generous subsidies to Cuba, forced Castro to liberalize some economic policies. The Cuban economy eventually began to improve through trade with Latin America. Castro remained president until his resignation in 2008.

Save the Cuban Revolution

" We built this revolution ourselves. No one built it for us. No one defended it for us. No one saved it for us. We did it ourselves. We defended it ourselves. We saved it ourselves and we will continue to do so. We will continue to defend it and we will continue to save it as often as necessary. "

" Our moral values and revolutionary principles helped us send over 300,000 internationalist combatants. No other country in the world has done that. Those values must be present now. This country is now required to express its internationalism; it is required to conduct an extraordinary internationalist mission: to save the Cuban Revolution; to save socialism in Cuba. "

" The revolutionary ideas are not defeated ... They are going through hard times, but they will return. And the more injustice there is in the world, the faster they will return. The more exploitation there is in the world, the more hunger there is in the world, the more chaos there is in the world, the faster the revolutionary ideas will return. "

" We, who are the standard bearers of these ideas, must hold them up. History has given us this mission ... we have the intelligence, the moral virtue, courage, and heroism to carry out that mission. "

Castro with Soviet premier Nikita Khrushchev in 1960. Khrushchev promised Castro in May 1960 to defend Cuba with Soviet arms. In October 1962, President John F. Kennedy blockaded Cuba after learning of Soviet nuclear-armed missiles on the island. Khrushchev agreed to dismantle the missiles in Cuba in exchange for Kennedy committing the U.S. never to invade Cuba.

ANITA HILL

October 11, 1991

In one of the most famous "he said, she said" incidents in American history, University of Oklahoma law professor Anita Hill testified before the Senate Judiciary Committee in 1991 that she had been the victim of prolonged sexual harassment by her former supervisor, then-Supreme Court nominee Clarence Thomas. Thomas categorically denied the allegations, describing Hill's testimony as "a high-tech lynching for uppity blacks."

Thomas, a conservative lawyer who had served in the U.S. Department of Education and the Equal Employment Opportunity Commission, was President George H. W. Bush's pick to replace a retiring Supreme Court Justice. During the Senate confirmation hearings, Hill calmly detailed how Thomas repeatedly asked her on dates, commented on her sexual attractiveness, and described his own sexual life as well as acts he had witnessed in pornographic films.

Although Hill endured public ridicule and Thomas has remained on the Supreme Court, the hearings brought light to the issue of sexual harassment in the workplace. Hill's testimony also helped inspire several women to run successfully for Senate seats the following year.

> " He made a comment that I will vividly remember. He said that if I ever told anyone of his behavior that it would ruin his career. This was not an apology, nor was it an explanation. "

Senate Judiciary Committee Testimony

"What happened next and telling the world about it are the two most difficult things—experiences of my life. It is only after a great deal of agonizing consideration and a great number of sleepless nights that I am able to talk of these unpleasant matters to anyone but my close friends."

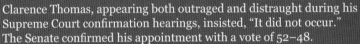

Clarence Thomas, appearing both outraged and distraught during his Supreme Court confirmation hearings, insisted, "It did not occur." The Senate confirmed his appointment with a vote of 52–48.

"I declined any comment to newspapers, but later when Senate staff asked me about these matters I felt I had a duty to report. I have no personal vendetta against Clarence Thomas. I seek only to provide the committee with information which it may regard as relevant."

"It would have been more comfortable to remain silent . . . But when I was asked by a representative of this committee to report my experience, I felt that I had to tell the truth. I could not keep silent."

Pat Buchanan, a journalist who had worked for Presidents Richard Nixon, Gerald Ford, and Ronald Reagan, made his first unsuccessful run for the Republican presidential nomination in 1992. Although he lost to incumbent President George H. W. Bush, the nearly 3 million votes he garnered earned him the podium on opening night at the Republican National Convention in Houston.

In his speech Buchanan drew on themes introduced the preceding year by sociologist James Davison Hunter in his book *Culture Wars: The Struggle to Define America*. Buchanan described an American public split into morally irreconcilable factions, bitterly divided over issues like abortion, gay rights, and prayer in school. The two groups were battling "for the soul of America," he said.

While Buchanan's notion of a culturally polarized country dominates media coverage, voter research consistently reveals that no such divide exists. The majority of Americans are "moderate" in their views, taking "conservative" positions on some issues and maintaining a "liberal" stance on others.

Buchanan delivering his "Cultural War" address.

PAT BUCHANAN

August 17, 1992

> " **We must take back our cities, and take back our culture, and take back our country.** "

Cultural War

Buchanan is shown here on the campaign trail during the Republican presidential primary in 1992.

" Friends, this election is about more than who gets what. It is about who we are. It is about what we believe and what we stand for as Americans. There is a religious war going on in this country. It is a cultural war, as critical to the kind of nation we shall be as the Cold War itself. For this war is for the soul of America. "

" The American people are not going to go back to the discredited liberalism of the 1960s and the failed liberalism of the 1970s, no matter how slick the package in 1992. "

" **George Bush is a defender of right-to-life, and a champion of the Judeo-Christian values and beliefs upon which America was founded.** "

" The agenda Clinton & Clinton would impose on America—abortion on demand, a litmus test for the Supreme Court, homosexual rights, discrimination against religious schools, women in combat units—that's change, all right. But it is not the kind of change America needs. It is not the kind of change America wants. And it is not the kind of change we can abide in a nation we still call God's country. "

Bush had famously promised, "Read my lips: No new taxes" during the 1988 election. Buchanan used the failed promise against him in the 1992 primary campaign.

MARY FISHER

August 19, 1992

Fisher delivering her convention speech.

The headlines following Mary Fisher's "A Whisper of AIDS" speech focused on the surprising effect she had on the milling midday throng at the 1992 Republican National Convention in Houston. "Hushed Delegates Hear from Woman with HIV," read the *San Francisco Chronicle*. *The New York Times* reported, "AIDS Speech Brings Hush to Crowd." At an event that kicked off with Pat Buchanan's polarizing "Cultural War" speech, her address was an unexpected triumph.

Fisher was a white, wealthy, heterosexual mother who had worked in the Gerald Ford administration and contracted HIV from her former husband. By presenting herself as a victim of AIDS, Fisher challenged the stereotypes that had prompted her party's platform to state with respect to the disease, "Prevention is linked ultimately to personal responsibility and moral behavior."

Her address and a similar one given by AIDS victim and activist Elizabeth Glaser at the Democratic National Convention that year helped to raise awareness and support for the struggle against HIV and AIDS.

> " I asked the Republican Party to lift the shroud of silence which has been draped over the issue of HIV and AIDS. I have come tonight to bring our silence to an end. I bear a message of challenge, not self-congratulation. I want your attention, not your applause. "

> " To all within the sound of my voice, I appeal: Learn with me the lessons of history and of grace, so my children will not be afraid to say the word "AIDS" when I am gone. Then, their children and yours may not need to whisper it at all. "

A Whisper of AIDS

> Tonight I represent an AIDS community whose members have been reluctantly drafted from every segment of American society. Though I am white and a mother, I am one with a black infant struggling with tubes in a Philadelphia hospital. Though I am female and contracted this disease in marriage and enjoy the warm support of my family, I am one with the lonely gay man sheltering a flickering candle from the cold wind of his family's rejection.

Fisher has continued to work as an AIDS activist, bringing attention to AIDS through speeches and art. She is shown here during a trip to South Africa in 2000.

The AIDS Memorial Quilt began in 1987. It has continued to grow over the years as people create and send in new panels as memorials for those who have died of the disease. This photograph shows the last display of the full quilt in Washington, D.C., in 1996.

> Tonight HIV marches resolutely toward AIDS in more than a million American homes, littering its pathway with the bodies of the young—young men, young women, young parents, and young children. One of the families is mine. If it is true that HIV inevitably turns to AIDS, then my children will inevitably turn to orphans.

> To the millions of you who are grieving, who are frightened, who have suffered the ravages of AIDS firsthand: Have courage, and you will find support. To the millions who are strong, I issue the plea: Set aside prejudice and politics to make room for compassion and sound policy.

TONI MORRISON

December 7, 1993

After becoming the first African American ever to win the Nobel Prize for Literature, Toni Morrison took the podium at the Swedish Academy in Stockholm and mesmerized her crowd with a speech about the power of language.

Morrison began her lecture with a folk tale: Some children decide to play a trick on an old blind woman. One of them says he has a bird in his hands and asks her if it is living or dead. After a long silence, the old woman says, "I don't know whether the bird you are holding is dead or alive, but what I do know is that it is in your hands."

Morrison said she chose to read the bird as language and the woman as a writer. Throughout her lecture, Morrison stressed the power of language to oppress or liberate. Morrison's speech revealed her view of the role of language and the responsibilities of those who wield it.

Toni Morrison in 2009.

> " Oppressive language does more than represent violence; it is violence; does more than represent the limits of knowledge; it limits knowledge . . . whether it is the malign language of law-without-ethics, or language designed for the estrangement of minorities, hiding its racist plunder in its literary cheek—it must be rejected, altered, and exposed. "

The Power of Language

> Sexist language, racist language, theistic language—all are typical of the policing languages of mastery, and cannot, do not permit new knowledge or encourage the mutual exchange of ideas.

> The vitality of language lies in its ability to limn the actual, imagined, and possible lives of its speakers, readers, writers. Although its poise is sometimes in displacing experience it is not a substitute for it. It arcs toward the place where meaning may lie.

> Language can never live up to life once and for all. Nor should it. Language can never "pin down" slavery, genocide, war. Nor should it yearn for the arrogance to be able to do so. Its force, its felicity is in its reach toward the ineffable.

> Be it grand or slender, burrowing, blasting, or refusing to sanctify; whether it laughs out loud or is a cry without an alphabet, the choice word, the chosen silence, unmolested language surges toward knowledge, not its destruction.

President Barack Obama awarded Toni Morrison the Presidential Medal of Freedom in 2012.

> We die. That may be the meaning of life. But we do language. That may be the measure of our lives.

Mother Teresa with children at an orphanage in Calcutta (now Kolkata), India, opened by her order. The Missionaries of Charity are active in over 130 countries.

MOTHER TERESA

February 3, 1994

Born Agnes Gonxha Bojaxhiu in Macedonia, Mother Teresa left home at age 18 to join an Irish missionary order that worked in India. After 17 years teaching in the organization's school in Calcutta (now Kolkata), she started her own program in the city's slums. The work she began grew into its own order, the Missionaries of Charity, dedicated to caring for the sick and destitute in India and elsewhere. She opened a home for the dying, a leper colony, and centers for people who were blind, aged, or disabled. As the Missionaries of Charity grew, Mother Teresa's name became synonymous with charity and self-sacrifice.

In her 1994 address at the National Prayer Breakfast in Washington, D.C., she spoke of the need to "give until it hurts, with a smile." She also addressed abortion in her speech, calling it "the greatest destroyer of peace today." Mother Teresa was also a vocal opponent of divorce and contraception.

Within two years of Mother Teresa's death in 1997, the process to declare her a saint was begun. Her beatification in 2003 was the quickest ever achieved in the Roman Catholic Church. Pope Francis I canonized her in 2016.

National Prayer Breakfast

The Chairman of the Nobel Institute awarding the Nobel Peace Prize to Mother Teresa in 1979 for her "work in bringing help to suffering humanity."

" It is not enough for us to say, "I love God," but I also have to love my neighbor. Saint John says that you are a liar if you say you love God and you don't love your neighbor. How can you love God whom you do not see, if you do not love your neighbor whom you see, whom you touch, with whom you live? And so it is very important for us to realize that love, to be true, has to hurt. I must be willing to give whatever it takes not to harm other people and, in fact, to do good to them. This requires that I be willing to give until it hurts. "

" There is so much hatred, so much misery, and we with our prayer, with our sacrifice, are beginning at home. Love begins at home, and it is not how much we do, but how much love we put into what we do. "

President Ronald Reagan presented Mother Teresa with the Presidential Medal of Freedom in 1985.

" I want you to find the poor here, right in your own home first. And begin love there. Be that good news to your own people first. "

GLORIA STEINEM

May 12, 1994

In her 1994 Ford Hall Forum speech and the question and answer session that followed, Gloria Steinem described the partial progress of the women's movement. She noted that while many people had come to accept the idea that women could do the jobs that had traditionally belonged to men, the reverse was not yet true. As a result, women had "two jobs instead of one," a salaried career as well as the family's domestic and childrearing responsibilities. Steinem predicted that just as it had taken America 150 years to give women "a legal identity," it would likely take another 100 years to achieve "legal and social equality."

Steinem, one of the central figures in the 20th-century women's liberation movement, helped transform the role of women in American society. She was involved in founding the National Women's Political Caucus and the Coalition of Labor Union Women. These and other political organizing efforts contributed to the passage of laws against gender discrimination in areas like employment and the use of federal funds.

Steinem is shown here during a 2004 Planned Parenthood Advocacy event.

In 1972, Steinem cofounded *Ms.* magazine, the first publication devoted to bringing a feminist perspective to investigative journalism and political analysis.

Moving Beyond Words

> " The first thing may be to say, 'I'm a feminist.' Because then people who love you will begin to think differently about feminism. "

Steinem in 1970. The following year, Steinem helped found the National Women's Political Caucus, dedicated to recruiting and supporting women seeking political office. On a speech given on that occasion, she said, "Sex and race, because they are easy, visible differences, have been the primary ways of organizing human beings into superior and inferior groups and into the cheap labor on which this system still depends."

President Barack Obama awarded Steinem the Presidential Medal of Freedom at a ceremony at the White House in 2013.

Steinem in 1970, two years before the founding of *Ms.* magazine.

NEWT GINGRICH

January 4, 1995

After 40 years of Democratic control in the U.S. House of Representatives, Republicans won control of both houses of Congress in 1994. Their successful campaign strategy, engineered by Georgia Representative Newt Gingrich, involved a "Contract with America" specifying legislative action the House would take if Republicans won a majority. The contract included such items as congressional term limits, an executive line-item veto, welfare reforms, tax cuts, a balanced budget, and a professional audit of congressional spending. Republican candidates promised to bring each of the proposals to a vote within 100 days if elected. As a result, Republicans gained 54 seats in the House and eight seats in the Senate. The power shift became known as the "Republican Revolution."

Gingrich became Speaker of the House and promised in his opening address to fulfill the "Contract with America." With the exception of the provision for term limits, the House succeeded in its ambitious legislative agenda. Most of the items, however, were voted down in the Senate or vetoed by President Bill Clinton.

Gingrich addressing the opening session of the 104th Congress on January 4.

Opening Address to the 104th Congress

> **Our challenge shouldn't be to balance the budget, to pass the Contract. Our challenge shouldn't be anything that's just legislative. We're supposed to, each one of us, be leaders.**

The "Contract with America" was presented on September 27, 1994, and was signed by almost all Republican members of the House of Representatives and Republican candidates who aspired to office. President Bill Clinton quipped that it was the "Contract on America."

> We must replace the welfare state with an opportunity society.

> The choice becomes not just do you want more or do you want less, but are there ways to do it better? Can we learn from the private sector?

> I would say to my friends on the left who believe there has never been a government program that was not worth keeping, you cannot look at some of the results we now have and not want to reach out to the humans and forget the bureaucracies.

Gingrich and other members of Congress met with Clinton on January 5, 1995. Later that year the two men would clash over the federal budget, leading to a shutdown of government services deemed non-essential and tarnishing Gingrich's reputation.

WILLIAM J. CLINTON

April 23, 1995

On April 19, 1995, Oklahoma City's Alfred P. Murrah Federal Building was torn apart by the explosion of a massive homemade bomb hidden inside a rental truck. The blast killed 168 people, 19 of whom were children, and injured another 500. Until the September 11, 2001 attacks, the Oklahoma City bombing was the deadliest terrorist attack on American soil. It remains the deadliest act of domestic terrorism in the nation's history.

Law enforcement quickly identified U.S. Army veteran Timothy McVeigh as the primary architect of the bombing, and his friend Terry Nichols as a co-conspirator. McVeigh planned the attack to coincide with the anniversary of the FBI's 1993 siege of the Branch Davidian religious compound in Waco, Texas. McVeigh's actions were intended to "wake up people" to the sinister actions of the government.

President Bill Clinton spoke at a memorial service four days after the attack. He pledged to "do all we can to help you heal the injured, to rebuild this city, and to bring to justice those who did this evil."

> **Today our nation joins with you in grief. We mourn with you. We share your hope against hope that some may still survive... We pledge to do all we can to help you heal the injured, to rebuild this city, and to bring to justice those who did this evil.**

Oklahoma City Bombing Memorial Address

> " You have lost too much, but you have not lost everything. And you have certainly not lost America, for we will stand with you for as many tomorrows as it takes. "

President Bill Clinton declared April 23 a national day of mourning, and he and Hillary Rodham Clinton both attended the memorial prayer service in Oklahoma City. Police had already arrested McVeigh at that point, and Nichols was being questioned.

Within minutes of the bombing, a massive search-and-rescue effort began that included fire, emergency, medical, and law enforcement personnel. The federal response to the incident included increased investigations into domestic militia movements and extremist groups.

> " To all my fellow Americans beyond this hall, I say, one thing we owe those who have sacrificed is the duty to purge ourselves of the dark forces which gave rise to this evil. They are forces that threaten our common peace, our freedom, our way of life. "

> " Let us let our own children know that we will stand against the forces of fear. When there is talk of hatred, let us stand up and talk against it. When there is talk of violence, let us stand up and talk against it. In the face of death, let us honor life. "

HILLARY CLINTON

September 5, 1995

The United Nations convened its Fourth World Conference on Women in 1995. The conference focused on the advancement of women in relation to such concerns as health care, poverty, violence, and civic representation. American delegate and First Lady Hillary Rodham Clinton delivered the most memorable speech of the conference. Stating, "Women's rights are human rights," she listed examples of the abuses that women and girls suffer across the world, including rape as a war tactic, genital mutilation, and slave trafficking.

Clinton's speech and the conference as a whole helped to galvanize efforts to end human rights abuses and to improve women's access to education, health care, economic opportunities, and positions in public office. The address also raised Clinton's profile, aiding her advocacy efforts within her husband's administration and helping her win a Senate seat in 2000 and the position of Secretary of State under President Barack Obama in 2008.

Women's Rights Are Human Rights

" The great challenge of this conference is to give voice to women everywhere whose experiences go unnoticed, whose words go unheard. Women comprise more than half the world's population, 70% of the world's poor, and two-thirds of those who are not taught to read and write. We are the primary caretakers for most of the world's children and elderly. Yet much of the work we do is not valued—not by economists, not by historians, not by popular culture, not by government leaders. "

" We need to understand there is no one formula for how women should lead our lives. That is why we must respect the choices that each woman makes for herself and her family. Every woman deserves the chance to realize her own God-given potential. But we must recognize that women will never gain full dignity until their human rights are respected and protected. "

Clinton in February 2010, visiting Saudi Arabia in her role as Secretary of State.

" If there is one message that echoes forth from this conference, let it be that human rights are women's rights and women's rights are human rights once and for all. Let us not forget that among those rights are the right to speak freely—and the right to be heard. "

" Let me be clear. Freedom means the right of people to assemble, organize, and debate openly. It means respecting the views of those who may disagree with the views of their governments. It means not taking citizens away from their loved ones and jailing them, mistreating them, or denying them their freedom or dignity because of the peaceful expression of their ideas and opinions. "

THABO MBEKI

May 8, 1996

South African deputy president Thabo Mbeki commemorated the initial passage of the country's new constitution with a speech before the Constitutional Assembly in Cape Town in 1996. His poetic address recounted parts of the region's history, claiming that even the most violent episodes were fundamental elements of African identity. Mbeki was similarly inclusive toward the people of Africa, describing immigrants from Europe and Asia as contributors to African lineage. In reference to the significance of the constitution's acceptance, he said, "Today it feels good to be an African."

The speech was remarkable not only for its powerful imagery but also its unlikely source—the shy, scholarly Mbeki. As deputy president under Nelson Mandela, Mbeki had been a cool, calculating intellectual in contrast to Mandela's warm, engaging persona. Mbeki's speech helped reveal a passionate and sensitive side of Mbeki, who went on to succeed Mandela as president in 1999.

> **I am an African. I owe my being to the hills and the valleys, the mountains and the glades, the rivers, the deserts, the trees, the flowers, the seas, and the ever-changing seasons that define the face of our native land.**

> I am formed of the migrants who left Europe to find a new home on our native land. Whatever their own actions, they remain still part of me.

Mbeki was sworn in as president in Pretoria in June 1999. He was reelected in 2004.

I Am an African

Thabo Mbeki and F. W. de Klerk shared the role of deputy president during the first two years of Nelson Mandela's presidency. Mbeki continued in the office alone for several more years after de Klerk left in 1996.

" I owe my being to the Khoi and the San whose desolate souls haunt the great expanses of the beautiful Cape—they who fell victim to the most merciless genocide our native land has ever seen, they who were the first to lose their lives in the struggle to defend our freedom and independence. "

" In my veins courses the blood of the Malay slaves who came from the East. Their proud dignity informs my bearing, their culture a part of my essence. The stripes they bore on their bodies from the lash of the slave master are a reminder embossed on my consciousness of what should not be done. "

" **The constitution whose adoption we celebrate constitutes an unequivocal statement that we refuse to accept that our African-ness shall be defined by our race, our color, our gender, or our historical origins.** "

" **I am born of a people who are heroes and heroines. I am born of a people who would not tolerate oppression. I am of a nation that would not allow that fear of death, of torture, of imprisonment, of exile or persecution should result in the perpetuation of injustice.** "

CHRISTOPHER REEVE

August 26, 1996

Christopher Reeve, the actor who played Superman in the block-buster film series, became quadriplegic after falling from a horse in 1995. Thereafter the person that so many recognized as the "man of steel" required both a wheelchair and a respirator. Reeve's high profile made him appear to be an obvious spokesperson for people with disabilities. The year after his accident, he was invited to give the closing speech at the 1996 Democratic National Convention in Chicago.

Early in the speech, Reeve called the 1990 Americans with Disabilities Act an important civil rights law that was "tearing down barriers." The remainder of his talk was devoted to his conviction that medical research could get "millions of people around the world like me up and out of these wheelchairs."

Reeve's talk was well received by the mainstream press and brought new attention to the prevalence of disability in America. But many in the disabled community felt that his focus on a "cure narrative" undermined their efforts by casting disability as a problem to be solved rather than a permanent situation meriting respectful accommodation.

Reeve delivering his speech at the Democratic National Convention in Chicago, Illinois.

Funding Medical Research

Our nation cannot tolerate discrimination of any kind. And that's why the Americans with Disabilities Act is so important. It must be honored everywhere. It is a civil rights law that is tearing down barriers, both in architecture and in attitude. Its purpose is to give the disabled access not only to buildings but to every opportunity in society.

One of the smartest things we can do about disability is to invest in research that will protect us from diseases and lead to cures.

The money we invest in research today is going to determine the quality of life of members of our family tomorrow.

Now that we know that nerves in the spinal cord can regenerate, we are on the way to getting millions of people around the world, millions of people around the world like me, up and out of these wheelchairs.

President Roosevelt showed us that a man who could barely lift himself out of a wheelchair could still lift this nation out of despair.

I believe, and so does this administration, in the most important principle that FDR taught us: America does not let its needy citizens fend for themselves. America is stronger when all of us take care of all of us. Giving new life to that ideal is the challenge before us tonight.

Reeve in 1996. He continued to advocate for research into spinal cord injuries until his death in 2004.

TONY BLAIR

August 31, 1997

When Diana, Princess of Wales, was killed in a car crash in Paris, British Prime Minister Tony Blair predicted, "The whole of our country, all of us, will be in a state of shock and mourning." Standing outside a church in county Durham, Blair captured the national sentiment in his hastily prepared speech.

Diana, who was married to the heir apparent Prince Charles from 1981 to 1996, was a beloved public figure. Even as her marriage publicly disintegrated, she continued to be seen as a generous person dedicated to charitable causes. Diana was also the most-photographed member of the royal family. The fatal crash occurred when she was fleeing the paparazzi. Her driver, who was also killed, was found to be primarily responsible for the accident, but the inquest determined that the paparazzi were also guilty of "gross negligence" that resulted in her death.

Blair explained in his statement, "I feel like everyone else in this country today—utterly devastated." The speech gave a boost to the newly elected prime minister's popularity.

Blair addressing the nation.

On Diana's Death

Diana, Princess of Wales, was known for her extensive charity work on a variety of causes. She is shown here visiting Bosnia-Herzegovina in August 1997, shortly before her death, in order to draw attention to the campaign against the use of land mines.

> **Diana was a wonderful, warm, and compassionate person who people, not just in Britain, but throughout the world, loved and will mourn as a friend.**

> Though her own life was often sadly touched by tragedy, she touched the lives of so many others in Britain—throughout the world—with joy and with comfort. How many times shall we remember her, in how many different ways, with the sick, the dying, with children, with the needy, when, with just a look or a gesture that spoke so much more than words, she would reveal to all of us the depth of her compassion and her humanity.

> She was the people's princess and that's how she will stay, how she will remain in our hearts and in our memories forever.

The United Kingdom mourned on an unprecedented scale. Large crowds gathered to bring flowers, candles, and cards to the gates of Kensington Palace in the wake of Diana's death.

Tutu presenting the TRC report to President Nelson Mandela. Upon receiving the report, Mandela said, "we should pay tribute to the 20,000 men and women who relived their pain and loss in order to share it with us; the hundreds who dared to open the wounds of guilt so as to exorcise it from the nation's body politic."

DESMOND TUTU

October 29, 1998

After Nelson Mandela became president of South Africa following the nation's first pan-ethnic election in 1994, his administration developed a Truth and Reconciliation Commission (TRC) to examine human rights violations committed during apartheid. The TRC was charged with developing "as complete a picture as possible of the nature, causes, and extent of gross violations of human rights" that occurred between 1960 and 1994. The commission could grant amnesty to perpetrators, propose reparations for victims, and recommend prosecution for those to whom it did not grant amnesty.

Cape Town Anglican Archbishop Desmond Tutu chaired the TRC. Tutu had been a high-profile anti-apartheid activist who advocated nonviolent protest. He presented the commission's report to Mandela in South Africa's executive capital Pretoria on October 29, 1998.

The 3,500-page report described South Africa's former government as the chief perpetrators of gross human rights violations, but also condemned abuses by anti-apartheid leaders and groups. Although critics charged the TRC was denying victims justice and reopening old wounds, the commission is generally viewed as a vital element of South Africa's transition to a racially inclusive democracy.

Truth and Reconciliation

"Fellow South Africans, accept this report as an indispensable way to healing. Let the waters of healing flow from Pretoria today to cleanse our land, to cleanse its people, and to bring unity and reconciliation. And holding hands together, black and white, we will stride together into the future. And looking at our past, we will commit ourselves: Never again!"

Tutu visited the U.S. in January 1986 to raise awareness about apartheid and urge economic sanctions. The organization TransAfrica gathered more than one million signatures of support for the anti-apartheid movement and presented this "freedom letter" to Tutu at a protest in Washington, D.C.

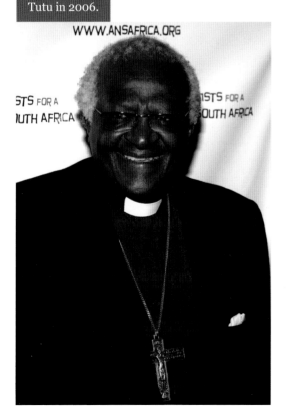

Tutu in 2006.

WWW.ANSAFRICA.ORG

RSA P W BOTHA 11c
Staatspresident 1984 State President

In ascribing blame for the abuses during the apartheid years, the TRC report concluded, "the preponderance of responsibility rests with the state and its allies." It specifically named former president Pieter W. Botha for overseeing a state security apparatus that planned, ordered, and committed killings, torture, abductions, arson, sabotage, and bombings from 1978–1989.

FREEDOM LETTERS

CHARLTON HESTON

February 16, 1999

Over his long career, actor Charlton Heston became synonymous with the stoic, steely-eyed heroes he portrayed. Although he was involved in civil rights activism in the 1960s, he later switched his political allegiance from the Democratic to the Republican Party. Heston declined to run for political office during the 1980s but later became involved with the National Rifle Association (NRA). He was elected the organization's president in 1998. He also began to speak publicly against "political correctness," famously asking a gathering of the Free Congress Foundation in 1997, "Why is 'Hispanic pride' or 'black pride' a good thing, while 'white pride' conjures up shaved heads and white hoods?"

The answer, he claimed, was "cultural warfare." In a speech at Harvard Law School in 1999 titled "Winning the Cultural War," he mocked the use of terms like "Native American" and "African American," and gave examples of specific sexual harassment policies, medical privacy laws, and ordinances protecting cross-dressers that he viewed as irrational intrusions into the private sphere. Conservative radio host Rush Limbaugh picked up the Harvard speech and read it on-air in its entirety. With the help of such publicity, many of Heston's statements became notable elements of right-wing political rhetoric.

Heston giving his speech at Harvard.

I believe that we are again engaged in a great civil war, a cultural war that's about to hijack your birthright to think and say what lives in your heart. I'm sure you no longer trust the pulsing lifeblood of liberty inside you, the stuff that made this country rise from wilderness into the miracle that it is.

Winning the Cultural War

"I've come to understand that a cultural war is raging across our land, in which, with Orwellian fervor, certain accepted thoughts and speech are mandated."

"If you talk about race, it does not make you a racist. If you see distinctions between the genders, it does not make you sexist. If you think critically about a denomination, it does not make you anti-religion. If you accept but don't celebrate homosexuality, it does not make you a homophobe. Don't let America's universities continue to serve as incubators for this rampant epidemic of new McCarthyism."

"How can anyone prevail against such pervasive social subjugation? ...You simply disobey. Peaceably, yes. Respectfully, of course. Nonviolently, absolutely. But when told how to think or what to say or how to behave, we don't. We disobey the social protocol that stifles and stigmatizes personal freedom."

"Disobedience is in our DNA. We feel innate kinship with that disobedient spirit that tossed tea into Boston Harbor, that sent Thoreau to jail, that refused to sit in the back of the bus, that protested a war in Vietnam. In that same spirit, I'm asking you to disavow cultural correctness with massive disobedience of rogue authority, social directives, and onerous laws that weaken personal freedom."

Heston is shown here at the NRA's 2003 annual convention. He was the NRA's president from 1998–2003. In his resignation speech, he brandished a rifle and said that gun control advocates could take it "from my cold, dead hands." Heston popularized the phrase at the 2000 NRA convention and used frequently thereafter.

ELIEZER WIESEL

April 12, 1999

Eliezer "Elie" Wiesel was 15 years old when his family was deported from Romania to the Auschwitz concentration camps in 1944. He and his father were sent to the slave labor sub-camp Buna-Monowitz, then marched to Buchenwald in January 1945. Wiesel's parents and younger sister were among the six million Jews who did not survive Nazi extermination efforts.

Wiesel's book *Night* about his Holocaust experience eventually became standard reading for high school and college classes. Wiesel wrote many more books about human suffering, received the Nobel Peace Prize in 1986, and served on a commission that created the United States Holocaust Memorial Museum.

President Bill Clinton and First Lady Hillary Clinton invited Wiesel to speak at the White House in 1999 as part of their Millennium Lecture Series. His talk, "The Perils of Indifference: Lessons Learned from a Violent Century," recounted some of the horrors he experienced at Auschwitz. The prisoners' only consolation during that time, he said, was the belief that the rest of the world was unaware of their plight. He stated, "If they knew, we thought, surely those leaders would have moved heaven and earth to intervene." Learning later that the U.S. government had, in fact, been aware of those atrocities before joining World War II taught him the dangers of indifference.

The U.S. Holocaust Memorial Museum dedication ceremony took place ten days after Wiesel's speech. Here Wiesel (right), Clinton (center), and the chairman of the U.S. Holocaust Council (left) light an eternal flame.

> "Indifference is always the friend of the enemy, for it benefits the aggressor—never his victim, whose pain is magnified when he or she feels forgotten. The political prisoner in his cell, the hungry children, the homeless refugees—not to respond to their plight, not to relieve their solitude by offering them a spark of hope is to exile them from human memory. And in denying their humanity we betray our own."

The Perils of Indifference

> " To be indifferent to that suffering is what makes the human being inhuman. Indifference, after all, is more dangerous than anger and hatred. Anger can at times be creative. One writes a great poem, a great symphony. One does something special for the sake of humanity because one is angry at the injustice that one witnesses. But indifference is never creative. Even hatred at times may elicit a response. You fight it. You denounce it. You disarm it. "

> " **In the place that I come from, society was composed of three simple categories: the killers, the victims, and the bystanders. During the darkest of times, inside the ghettoes and death camps . . . we felt abandoned, forgotten.** "

U.S. Army photographs documented the conditions in the concentration camps they liberated. In this photograph at Buchenwald, Wiesel appears in the second row from the bottom, seventh from the left.

President Barack Obama touring the U.S. Holocaust Memorial Museum in Washington, D.C., with museum director Sara Bloomfield (left) and Elie Wiesel (right) in 2012.

> " We believed that Auschwitz and Treblinka were closely guarded secrets; that the leaders of the free world did not know what was going on behind those black gates and barbed wire; that they had no knowledge of the war against the Jews that Hitler's armies and their accomplices waged as part of the war against the Allies. If they knew, we thought, surely those leaders would have moved heaven and earth to intervene. They would have spoken out with great outrage and conviction. "

Tim Berners-Lee delivering an address in January 2012.

TIM BERNERS-LEE

April 14, 1999

> " The basic idea of the Web is that an information space through which people can communicate, but communicate in a special way: communicate by sharing their knowledge in a pool. The idea was not just that it should be a big browsing medium. The idea was that everybody would be putting their ideas in, as well as taking them out. "

British computer scientist Tim Berners-Lee invented the World Wide Web, an Internet-based hypermedia initiative for global information sharing, while working at CERN, the European particle physics laboratory. Berners-Lee wrote the first Web server and the first Web client ("browser") between 1990 and 1991. On April 14, 1999, some 1,500 faculty, computer scientists, and tech leaders jammed a field house on the campus of Massachusetts Institute of Technology (MIT) eager to hear Berners-Lee wax poetic about the Internet.

Instead, Berners-Lee delivered a cautionary talk about how the Web, for all its power, was still in its crucial developing stages. He spoke about how it could fragment or even self-destruct if forces were allowed to restrict the information access now at the world's fingertips. The Web needed nurturing and guidance, he warned, from dedicated advocates around the globe. The result of such development, he said, could connect people in deep and meaningful ways across geographic, economic, political, and cultural boundaries.

The Evolution of the World Wide Web

> We don't just want to make something which works; we want to make something which can evolve.

> We need digital signature so that when you share things with your colleagues you know that you're sharing it with your colleagues and you're not sharing it with just anybody, any hacker who happened to turn up on that strip of Ethernet.

> People can solve problems intuitively. When people browse across the Web and see something expressed in natural language, they think, "Aha!" and suddenly solve a totally unrelated problem due to the incredible ability that the human brain has to spot a pattern totally out of context by a huge amount of parallel processing. It's very important that we use this human intuitive ability because everything else we can automate.

> For me the fundamental Web is the Web of people. It's not the Web of machines talking to each other...if we're not doing something for the Web of people, then we're really not doing something useful at all.

> I'm very interested in a more fractal, less hierarchical structure arising in society, allowing us to operate using the Web of trust. Perhaps we can, now that we've got machines that can help us find out individually where we best fit, how we can weave ourselves into the Web to contribute best to society.

This stamp from the Marshall Islands commemorates Tim Berners-Lee's revolutionary invention of the World Wide Web.

Berners-Lee in 2014 at the Webby Awards in New York City.

GEORGE W. BUSH

September 11, 2001

On September 11, 2001, Al Qaeda terrorists hijacked four passenger airplanes, crashing two of the planes into the twin towers of the World Trade Center in New York City and a third plane into the Pentagon. A fourth jet crashed in rural Pennsylvania when passengers and crew fought back against the hijackers. Nearly 3,000 people were killed, and thousands more were injured in the nation's deadliest terrorist attack.

President George W. Bush was visiting Emma E. Booker Elementary School in Sarasota, Florida, that morning when he learned of the attacks. In his first public remarks from the school, he said, "Today, we've had a national tragedy. Two airplanes have crashed into the World Trade Center in an apparent terrorist attack on our country." The president and his team weren't aware of any other hijacked or missing aircraft at that time. Back in Washington, D.C., that night, Bush delivered a televised address to the nation on the day's terrorist attacks and emphasized America's resolve.

President George W. Bush addressing the nation from the Oval Office on September 11.

 Today, our fellow citizens, our way of life, our very freedom came under attack in a series of deliberate and deadly terrorist acts.

9/11 Address to the Nation

Terrorists flew a passenger plane into the north tower of the World Trade Center at 8:46 a.m. Americans watched in horror as a second plane struck the south tower at 9:03 a.m.

"The pictures of airplanes flying into buildings, fires burning, huge structures collapsing have filled us with disbelief, terrible sadness, and a quiet, unyielding anger."

"Terrorist attacks can shake the foundations of our biggest buildings, but they cannot touch the foundation of America. These acts shatter steel, but they cannot dent the steel of American resolve."

"The search is underway for those who were behind these evil acts ... We will make no distinction between the terrorists who committed these acts and those who harbor them."

"Today, our nation saw evil—the very worst of human nature—and we responded with the best of America. With the daring of our rescue workers, with the caring for strangers and neighbors who came to give blood and help in any way they could."

On September 14, Bush visited Ground Zero workers and gave what is now called the "Bullhorn Address." A worker yelled, "I can't hear you!" Bush responded, "I can hear you! The rest of the world hears you! And the people who knocked these buildings down will hear all of us soon!"

Annan receiving his award.

> **No one today is unaware of this divide between the world's rich and poor. No one today can claim ignorance of the cost that this divide imposes on the poor and dispossessed who are no less deserving of human dignity, fundamental freedoms, security, food, and education than any of us. The cost, however, is not borne by them alone. Ultimately, it is borne by all of us.**

KOFI ANNAN

December 10, 2001

The 2001 Nobel Peace Prize was awarded jointly to the United Nations (UN) and to its Secretary-General, Kofi Annan. In his Nobel Lecture in Oslo, Annan described the interconnections between societies. Each individual's freedom and security hinged on meeting the UN's goals of "eradicating poverty, preventing conflict, and promoting democracy" worldwide.

Born in Ghana, Annan spent most of his career within the UN before becoming Secretary-General in 1997. During his two terms, Annan renewed the organization's commitment to global human rights. He focused attention on the HIV/AIDS crisis, adopted the UN's first counter-terrorism strategy, and developed new connections with corporations and other non-governmental agencies.

Although several UN departments and officials had previously been Peace Prize recipients, 2001 was the first time that the whole organization had been given the honor. Annan observed in his speech that the Nobel Peace Prize made a major impact on global peacekeeping efforts. "Sadly, a prize for peace is a rarity in this world," he said. "Most nations have monuments or memorials to war, bronze salutations to heroic battles, archways of triumph. But peace has no parade, no pantheon of victory."

> **Today's real borders are not between nations, but between powerful and powerless, free and fettered, privileged and humiliated.**

At a news conference in 1996, shortly before he took office as Secretary-General, Annan pledged to renew the United Nations.

> In the 21st century I believe the mission of the United Nations will be defined by a new, more profound awareness of the sanctity and dignity of every human life, regardless of race or religion. This will require us to look beyond the framework of states, and beneath the surface of nations or communities. We must focus, as never before, on improving the conditions of the individual men and women who give the state or nation its richness and character.

> Each of us has the right to take pride in our particular faith or heritage. But the notion that what is ours is necessarily in conflict with what is theirs is both false and dangerous. It has resulted in endless enmity and conflict, leading men to commit the greatest of crimes in the name of a higher power.

Annan, photographed here at the traditional torch-light parade held in honor of the Nobel Peace Prize laureate, remained in his role at the UN until 2006.

> Beneath the surface of states and nations, ideas and language, lies the fate of individual human beings in need. Answering their needs will be the mission of the United Nations in the century to come.

JANE GOODALL

March 2002

British primatologist and anthropologist Jane Goodall is considered the foremost expert on chimpanzees. Her research into chimpanzee behavior started in Africa in 1960 and continues today. Goodall founded a research institute in her name in 1977 and the Roots & Shoots program in 1991. Her work with animals has also lead her to become an environmentalist and conservationist. She noted that chimpanzees in the wild are "disappearing very fast" due to deforestation, encroachment by human populations, logging, mining, and the bush-meat trade.

In Goodall's 2002 TED talk, she described several similarities between humans and chimps, including the use of tools and non-verbal communication. Goodall said the only real difference between humans and chimps is our sophisticated spoken language. She challenged the crowd to start using that language to change the world. Leaving a light ecological footprint, she noted, would make the world a better place for humans, chimpanzees, and every other species.

> **We have found that after all, there isn't a sharp line dividing humans from the rest of the animal kingdom. It's a very wuzzy line. It's getting wuzzier all the time as we find animals doing things that we, in our arrogance, used to think was just human.**

Goodall speaking at the U.S. Department of the Interior headquarters in Washington, D.C., in November 2009.

What Separates Us from Chimpanzees?

Goodall travels with "Mr. H," her toy monkey and frequently brings him on stage when she speaks.

" We find chimps are capable of true compassion and altruism. We find in their non-verbal communication—this is very rich—they have a lot of sounds, which they use in different circumstances, but they also use touch, posture, gesture, and what do they do? They kiss; they embrace; they hold hands. They pat one another on the back; they swagger; they shake their fist—the kind of things that we do. "

" The one thing we have, which makes us so different from chimpanzees or other living creatures, is this sophisticated spoken language—a language with which we can tell children about things that aren't here. We can talk about the distant past, plan for the distant future, discuss ideas with each other, so that the ideas can grow from the accumulated wisdom of a group. "

" Once we're prepared to admit that after all, we're not the only beings with personalities, minds, and above all feelings, and then we start to think about ways we use and abuse so many other sentient, sapient creatures on this planet, it really gives cause for deep shame. "

" It's really up to us. We're the ones who can make a difference. If we lead lives where we consciously leave the lightest possible ecological footprints, if we buy the things that are ethical for us to buy and don't buy the things that are not, we can change the world overnight. "

Powell giving his presentation to the UN Security Council.

COLIN POWELL

February 5, 2003

"Iraq has now placed itself in danger of the serious consequences called for in UN Resolution 1441. And this body places itself in danger of irrelevance if it allows Iraq to continue to defy its will without responding effectively and immediately."

U.S. Secretary of State Colin Powell presented his case against Iraqi leader Saddam Hussein to the United Nations Security Council on February 5, 2003. Powell claimed Hussein had violated UN sanctions by concealing weapons of mass destruction. Using evidence that included audio recordings, satellite imagery, and eyewitness testimony, Powell described how Hussein was evacuating buildings prior to inspection, manufacturing chemical weapons in mobile laboratories, and collaborating with the terrorist group Al Qaeda.

The Security Council was not convinced that the intelligence called for action beyond the inspections program they already had underway. A number of world leaders including French president Jacques Chirac and German Chancellor Gerhard Schröder vocally opposed military action against Iraq.

Despite this lack of international support, President George W. Bush ordered U.S. forces to invade Iraq. Although they quickly toppled Hussein's regime, the invasion initiated a long and bloody struggle during which American troops and their allies became caught in a civil war. Later investigations revealed that most of Powell's assertions were false. Powell, a four-star general who had served in various White House positions for nearly 30 years, came to regard the speech as an unfortunate "blot" on his record.

UN Security Council Address on WMD in Iraq

> **The gravity of this moment is matched by the gravity of the threat that Iraq's weapons of mass destruction pose to the world.**

Baghdad on March 21, 2003, a day after the military invasion began. Although traditional combat operations came to a close on May 1, 2003, insurgency continued in the years that followed.

> Saddam Hussein has chemical weapons. Saddam Hussein has used such weapons. And Saddam Hussein has no compunction about using them again, against his neighbors and against his own people. And we have sources who tell us that he recently has authorized his field commanders to use them. He wouldn't be passing out the orders if he didn't have the weapons or the intent to use them.

> **Leaving Saddam Hussein in possession of weapons of mass destruction for a few more months or years is not an option, not in a post-September 11th world.**

Powell standing behind Bush in September 2003. Powell was asked to resign in late 2004.

> What I want to bring to your attention today is the potentially much more sinister nexus between Iraq and the Al Qaeda terrorist network, a nexus that combines classic terrorist organizations and modern methods of murder. Iraq today harbors a deadly terrorist network headed by Abu Musab Al-Zarqawi, an associate and collaborator of Osama bin Laden and his Al Qaeda lieutenants.

> Terrorism has been a tool used by Saddam for decades. Saddam was a supporter of terrorism long before these terrorist networks had a name. And this support continues. The nexus of poisons and terror is new. The nexus of Iraq and terror is old. The combination is lethal.

Obama giving his keynote speech.

BARACK OBAMA

July 27, 2004

The little-known Illinois state Senator Barack Obama took many by surprise with his keynote address at the 2004 Democratic National Convention in Boston. The speech would launch a national political career that took him first to the U.S. Senate and only four years later to the White House.

A Chicago lawyer and community organizer originally from Hawaii, Obama created a stir within the Democratic Party by winning his Senate primary in a landslide. His unusual lineage as the child of a Kenyan father and Kansas-born mother, combined with his progressive record and impressive oratorical skills, made him a standout among the party's rising stars.

In his keynote address, Obama shared his own story as "a skinny kid with a funny name." He focused on themes of hope and unity, which would later form the basis of his 2008 presidential campaign. With his win in 2008, Obama made history as the first African American to hold America's highest political office.

2004 DNC Keynote Address

 My parents shared not only an improbable love; they shared an abiding faith in the possibilities of this nation. They would give me an African name, Barack, or "blessed," believing that in a tolerant America your name is no barrier to success. They imagined me going to the best schools in the land, even though they weren't rich, because in a generous America you don't have to be rich to achieve your potential.

I stand here knowing that my story is part of the larger American story, that I owe a debt to all of those who came before me, and that, in no other country on Earth, is my story even possible.

Barack Obama became the first African American president of the Harvard Law Review in 1990. He went on to teach constitutional law at the University of Chicago.

Alongside our famous individualism, there's another ingredient in the American saga, a belief that we're all connected as one people ... It's what allows us to pursue our individual dreams and yet still come together as one American family.

Obama won his U.S. Senate seat in a landslide in November 2004 against Republican Alan Keyes.

There are those who are preparing to divide us—the spin masters, the negative ad peddlers who embrace the politics of "anything goes." Well, I say to them tonight, there is not a liberal America and a conservative America—there is the United States of America. There is not a Black America and a White America and Latino America and Asian America—there's the United States of America.

GERRY ADAMS

April 6, 2005

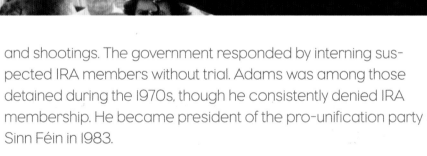

Gerry Adams at a rally in the summer of 1996.
The IRA had broken a ceasefire of 17 months
in February 1996 when peace talks foundered.
A summer filled with riots, carjackings, and
violence followed.

Irish nationalist leader Gerry Adams, president of the Sinn Féin political party, addressed the Irish Republican Army (IRA) in a speech in Belfast in 2005. He urged the IRA, which sought to protect the interests of Catholics and unify British-controlled Northern Ireland with the Irish Republic, to commit to a permanent policy of nonviolence. A few months later, IRA leaders announced that they had accepted Adams's proposal, pledging to end the armed struggle that had torn apart the region for decades.

During the period of violence between pro-unification Catholics and overwhelmingly Protestant British loyalists known as "the Troubles" (1960s–late 1990s), IRA tactics included bombings and shootings. The government responded by interning suspected IRA members without trial. Adams was among those detained during the 1970s, though he consistently denied IRA membership. He became president of the pro-unification party Sinn Féin in 1983.

Adams organized negotiations with both political rivals and international allies. His efforts led to the Good Friday Agreement of 1998, which provided for some measure of self-government in Northern Ireland. The IRA was still unwilling, however, to disarm completely. With his plea for peace in 2005, Adams set in motion the power-sharing process that at last created stability in the fractured country.

Appeal to the IRA

In November 1995, Adams noted that the current round of peace talks were in precarious shape. That round of peace talks did break down, and it would be more than a decade before the IRA would call for "an end to the armed campaign."

> " I have defended the right of the IRA to engage in armed struggle. I did so because there was no alternative for those who would not bend the knee, or turn a blind eye to oppression, or for those who wanted a national republic. Now there is an alternative. "

> " The way forward is by building political support for republican and democratic objectives across Ireland and by winning support for these goals internationally. "

> " I am asking you to join me in seizing this moment, to intensify our efforts, to rebuild the peace process, and decisively move our struggle forward. "

Carjackings and car bombings were common tactics used by paramilitary groups during "the Troubles." Here, youths set fire to a hijacked van.

In his speech to the Federalist Society, Karl Rove argued that "One of George W. Bush's greatest contributions as president will be the changes he's brought about in our courts."

> " In America, conservatives are winning the battle of ideas on almost every front, and few are more important than the battle over our judiciary. The outcome of that debate will shape the course of human events. "

KARL ROVE

November 10, 2005

Karl Rove, President George W. Bush's Deputy Chief of Staff, was often described as the brains behind the president. He orchestrated the campaigns that took Bush first to the Texas governor's mansion and then to the White House. Bush referred to Rove as "the architect." Rove's campaign tactics were so ruthless in their attempts to discredit Bush's political opponents that the term "Rovian" came to describe any campaign that relied on fear and smear to defeat the opposition.

In November 2005, Rove made an address to the Federalist Society in Washington, D.C. His talk focused on the Federalist Society's governing commitment to prevent "judicial activists" from interpreting the Constitution in light of current ethical standards rather than those of the Founding Fathers. In true Rovian style, he cast the issue as black-and-white, good-versus-evil, with "judicial imperialism" threatening to undermine self-government in a national "battle of ideas" between conservative and liberal factions.

Address to the Federalist Society

"America's 43rd president believes, as you do, that judges should base their opinions on strictly and faithfully interpreting the text of our Constitution, a document that is remarkable and reliable."

"Critics of constitutionalism say it is resistant to social change, our Constitution. But if the people want to enact or repeal certain laws, they can do so by persuading their fellow citizens on the merits through legislation or constitutional amendment. This makes eminent good sense, and it allows for enormous adaptability."

Bush and Rove during a July 2005 cabinet meeting. Rove left his role as Bush's Deputy Chief of Staff and Senior Advisor in August 2007.

"The Founders believed the role of the judiciary was vital, but also modest. They envisioned judges as impartial umpires, charged with guarding the sanctity of the Constitution, not as legislators dressed conveniently in robes."

"The Federalist Society is one of America's most important intellectual movements. Since your founding more than 20 years ago, you have made extraordinary efforts to return our country to constitutionalism."

Rove with Bush in 1994, after Bush's election to the governor's mansion.

HUGO CHÁVEZ

September 20, 2006

Venezuelan president Hugo Chávez made headlines when he described U.S. President George W. Bush as "the Devil" before the United Nations General Assembly in 2006. He went on to claim, "the American empire is doing all it can to consolidate its system of domination" and to call U.S. actions in the Middle East "fascist" and "genocidal."

The United States and Venezuela had once enjoyed good diplomatic relations, but with Chávez's election in 1998 and Bush's in 2000, the two nations set themselves on divergent political paths. Chávez aspired toward a socialist political system like Cuba's. Bush, meanwhile, was committed to "the growth of democratic movements and institutions in every nation and culture." Chávez had previously criticized Bush's invasion of Afghanistan following the September 11 attacks. He also allied Venezuela with Iraq, Iran, and Libya, causing further distance with the United States.

Chávez alienated many of his own people as well by claiming progressively greater powers for himself and dismantling the independent press. U.S.-Venezuela relations remained strained after Bush's departure from the White House. Chávez repeatedly likened Obama to a gun-slinging "cowboy" and blamed the U.S. for the disastrous 2010 earthquake in Haiti.

Address to the UN General Assembly

> **The Devil came here yesterday. Yesterday the Devil came here. Right here. And it smells of sulfur still.**

> The American empire is doing all it can to consolidate its system of domination. And we cannot allow them to do that. We cannot allow world dictatorship to be consolidated.

Chávez was briefly ousted in April 2002 after a series of violent protests. Chávez claimed the U.S. had been involved in planning the coup, which the Bush administration denied.

> They say they want to impose a democratic model. But that's their democratic model. It's the false democracy of elites, and, I would say, a very original democracy that's imposed by weapons and bombs.

> The hegemonic pretensions of the American empire are placing at risk the very survival of the human species. We continue to warn you about this danger and we appeal to the people of the United States and the world to halt this threat, which is like a sword hanging over our heads.

Supporters greeted Chávez as he returned to the presidential palace. He also survived a 2004 referendum attempting to recall him from power. Chávez remained president of Venezuela until his death in 2013.

BILL GATES

June 7, 2007

Microsoft cofounder Bill Gates spoke to the graduating class at Harvard University in 2007, one year before leaving his company to focus full-time on philanthropy. Gates attended Harvard for two years in the 1970s before dropping out to create software for the first personal computers. In his speech he recalled the exhilarating intellectual environment during his time at the university. But he also stated, "I left Harvard with no real awareness of the awful inequities in the world—the appalling disparities of health, and wealth, and opportunity that condemn millions of people to lives of despair."

He challenged the class of 2007 to use their greater awareness of global inequities to make meaningful changes rather than just making money. Gates told graduates, "When you consider what those of us here in this yard have been given—in talent, privilege, and opportunity—there is almost no limit to what the world has a right to expect from us."

Harvard Commencement Address

> " Humanity's greatest advances are not in its discoveries—but in how those discoveries are applied to reduce inequity. Whether through democracy, strong public education, quality health care, or broad economic opportunity—reducing inequity is the highest human achievement. "

> " The barrier to change is not too little caring; it is too much complexity. To turn caring into action, we need to see a problem, see a solution, and see the impact. "

Gates addressing the 2006 International Consumer Electronics Show. Gates's software programs, including Windows and Internet Explorer, changed the face of computing and paved the way for the digital revolution.

Bill and Melinda Gates opening the 16th International AIDS conference in 2006. Their foundation funds health, education, and antipoverty programs.

> " Cutting through complexity to find a solution runs through four predictable stages: determine a goal, find the highest-leverage approach, discover the ideal technology for that approach, and in the meantime, make the smartest application of the technology that you already have—whether it's something sophisticated, like a drug, or something simpler, like a bed net. "

> " I hope you will come back here to Harvard 30 years from now and reflect on what you have done with your talent and your energy. I hope you will judge yourselves not on your professional accomplishments alone, but also on how well you have addressed the world's deepest inequities, on how well you treated people a world away who have nothing in common with you but their humanity. "

CHRIS DODD

October 26, 2007

> **The damage that was done to our country on 9/11 was stunning. We all know it. It changed the world forever. But when you start diminishing our rights as a people, you compound that tragedy.**

On the floor of the U.S. Senate, Connecticut Senator Chris Dodd voiced his opposition to a proposed bill that would grant retroactive immunity to telecommunications companies that had participated in the National Security Administration's secret surveillance program under President George W. Bush. In his speech, Dodd contended that the surveillance program, like other Bush administration counter-terrorism efforts, weakened national security by sacrificing civil liberties and tarnishing America's international reputation.

The bill was intended to update the Foreign Intelligence Surveillance Act (FISA), passed in 1978 in response to revelations about widespread abuse of government wiretaps. The act created a secret court that could issue warrants for the purpose of collecting information related to foreign powers. The Bush administration never sought the court's approval for its activities, later insisting that the September 11 attacks had rendered FISA obsolete.

In 2005 *The New York Times* revealed Bush's "warrantless wiretapping" program, which included monitoring the phone calls and emails of American citizens. The disclosure sparked a national debate about privacy, security, and the rule of law. A critical element in the discussion was the role of the telecommunications companies who had complied with the National Security Administration's requests to turn over records in violation of existing privacy laws.

Senate Floor Speech on FISA

" Many of the unprecedented rollbacks of the rule of law by this administration have been made in the name of "national security." The Bush administration has relentlessly focused our nation's resources and manpower on a war of choice in Iraq. The ill-conceived war has broken our military, squandered our resources, and emboldened our enemies. "

" President Bush is right about one thing: The debate is about security but not in the way he imagines it, Mr. President. He believes we have to give up certain rights to be safer. I believe the choice between moral authority and security is a false choice. I believe it is precisely when you stand up and protect your rights that you become stronger, not weaker, as a nation. "

Like Hillary Clinton and Joe Biden, Dodd was a candidate in the 2008 Democratic presidential primary.

" You cannot protect America in the long run if you fail to protect our Constitution. It's that simple. "

" For six years this president has used scare tactics, in my view, to prevent the Congress from reining in his abuse of authority. A case in point is the current direction this body appears to be headed as we prepare to reform and extend the Foreign Intelligence Surveillance Act. "

President Obama meeting with Barney Frank, Dick Durbin, and Dodd at the White House prior to a financial regulatory reform announcement in June 2009. President Obama signed the Dodd-Frank Wall Street Reform and Consumer Protection Act into law in July 2010.

AL GORE

December 10, 2007

Al Gore, who served as vice president of the United States from 1993–2001, won the Nobel Peace Prize in 2007 for his work on global climate change and environmental protection. He shared the award with the United Nations Intergovernmental Panel on Climate Change, a global network of scientists investigating changes to the earth's climate and how human activities are contributing to these shifts. In his acceptance speech in Oslo, Gore reiterated the urgency of responding to the threat posed by increasing temperatures due to human degradation of the environment.

Gore had championed environmental causes during his earlier political career, when he represented his home state of Tennessee in Congress. After an unsuccessful bid for the presidency in 2000, when he lost the Electoral College to George W. Bush, he devoted most of his time to raising awareness about global warming. His 2006 documentary, *An Inconvenient Truth*, won an Academy Award and brought the issue to prominent national attention.

In his Nobel lecture, Gore specifically called for the United States and China to "make the boldest moves" in the pursuit for change.

Global Warming Nobel Lecture

" We, the human species, are confronting a planetary emergency, a threat to the survival of our civilization that is gathering ominous and destructive potential even as we gather here. But there is hopeful news as well: we have the ability to solve this crisis and avoid the worst—though not all—of its consequences, if we act boldly, decisively and quickly. "

" The earth has a fever. And the fever is rising. The experts have told us it is not a passing affliction that will heal by itself. We asked for a second opinion. And a third. And a fourth. And the consistent conclusion, restated with increasing alarm, is that something basic is wrong. We are what is wrong, and we must make it right. "

An Inconvenient Truth won an Oscar for Best Documentary in February 2007. On that occasion, Gore called climate change "not a political issue," but a "moral issue."

" Unlike most other forms of pollution, CO_2 is invisible, tasteless, and odorless—which has helped keep the truth about what it is doing to our climate out of sight and out of mind. Moreover, the catastrophe now threatening us is unprecedented—and we often confuse the unprecedented with the improbable. "

" We must quickly mobilize our civilization with the urgency and resolve that has previously been seen only when nations mobilized for war. These prior struggles for survival were won when leaders found words at the 11th hour that released a mighty surge of courage, hope, and readiness to sacrifice for a protracted and mortal challenge... Now comes the threat of climate crisis—a threat that is real, rising, imminent, and universal. Once again, it is the 11th hour. "

" We must abandon the conceit that individual, isolated, private actions are the answer. They can and do help. But they will not take us far enough without collective action. "

Michelle Obama addressing the Democratic National Convention.

MICHELLE OBAMA

August 25, 2008

Barack Obama's nomination as the Democratic presidential candidate in 2008 brought with it the prospect of the first African American First Lady. Michelle Obama, a lawyer with degrees from Harvard and Princeton who held high-level positions with University of Chicago Hospitals, noted this watershed moment in her address to the Democratic National Convention in Denver.

Michelle Obama was, for many voters, more accessible than Barack. While he grew up in Hawaii and drew his African lineage from a Kenyan father, Michelle was raised on the South Side of Chicago and traced her African heritage back to a great-great-great grandmother who was a slave. Many women related to her story of juggling a career while raising her two daughters and attempting to stay involved in her community.

After moving to the White House, Michelle was celebrated both for her fashion sense and for her dedication to causes ranging from childhood obesity to support for military families and promoting arts education.

> " This week we celebrate two anniversaries: the 88th anniversary of women winning the right to vote and the 45th anniversary of that hot summer day when Dr. King lifted our sights and our hearts with his dream for our nation. And I stand here today at the cross-currents of that history, knowing that my piece of the American dream is a blessing hard-won by those who came before me. "

DNC Keynote Address

In February 2010, Barack Obama signed a memorandum setting up a task force on childhood obesity, one of Michelle Obama's causes. On the same day, Michelle Obama launched her "Let's Move" campaign.

> **I believe that each of us—no matter what our age or background or our walk in life—each of us has something to contribute to the life of this nation.**

First Lady Michelle Obama spoke at the 2016 Democratic National Convention in Philadelphia, saying, "don't let anyone ever tell you that this country isn't great, that somehow we need to make it great again." She endorsed and campaigned for Democratic presidential candidate Hillary Clinton.

> We have an obligation to fight for the world as it should be. And that is the thread that connects our hearts. That is the thread that runs through my journey and Barack's journey and so many other improbable journeys that have brought us here tonight, where the current of history meets this new tide of hope.

The President and First Lady at an inaugural ball on January 20, 2009. Michelle is noted for her fashion sense and has appeared on many best-dressed lists.

> Barack doesn't care where you're from or what your background is or what party, if any, you belong to. See, that's just not how he sees the world. He knows that thread that connects us: our belief in America's promise, our commitment to our children's future—he knows that that thread is strong enough to hold us together as one nation even when we disagree.

Nader reiterated many of the themes from his October 4 speech on October 16, when he addressed a rally in front of the New York Stock Exchange.

RALPH NADER

October 4, 2008

When Congress passed the Emergency Economic Stabilization Act of 2008, a number of people protested. Some of them wrote newspaper articles describing the federal government's $700 billion bailout of the failing financial industry as anti-free-market "lemon socialism." Others gathered in the streets outside the New York Stock Exchange and the White House to demonstrate against using taxpayer money to reward irresponsible behavior. Ralph Nader, well-known consumer advocate and four-time presidential candidate, made a number of speeches decrying the legislation. Addressing a gathering in Waterbury, Connecticut, he called the bailout "taxation without representation" and likened President George W. Bush to King George III of England. Nader accused policymakers of backroom dealings. He lamented the lost opportunity to reinstitute regulations that were dismantled during the 1980s.

The legislation was passed in response to the subprime mortgage crisis, in which banks had made unprecedented numbers of high-risk loans that led to widespread mortgage delinquencies and foreclosures. The real estate crisis had a domino effect on the economy as lenders, investment banks, and hedge funds began to collapse. Government leaders who supported the bailout argued that the financial institutions involved were "too big to fail." Unless the government came to the rescue, they argued, the U.S. economy would enter a catastrophic decline.

Campaign Speech on the Bailout

> " The degradation of our democratic processes has hit a new low historically. There used to be a time when Congress would stand up to a president. Forget that. King George the Fourth is in charge. There used to be a time when Congress would never bail out a corrupt industry or a mismanaged industry on the backs of the taxpayers. Forget that. They've been doing it for years. "

In May 2008 Nader's campaign organized a protest against price gouging of gasoline in front of the American Petroleum Institute in Washington, D.C. The announcement promised further protests in "corporate occupied territory" as the campaign continued.

Polls showed that many Americans shared Nader's views on the bailout, but when election day came one month after his speech they gave him only 0.5 percent of the popular vote.

In his campaign speech, Nader accused policymakers of backroom dealings, pointing out that Treasury Secretary Henry Paulson (shown here with President Bush) was a former CEO of global investment firm Goldman Sachs.

MIKE MULLEN

February 2, 2010

Speaking at a hearing of the Senate Armed Services Committee, Admiral Mike Mullen, Chairman of the Joint Chiefs of Staff, became the highest-ranking active-duty officer to voice support for lifting the ban on gay people serving openly in the military. He described the issue as a matter of "integrity."

Mullen testifying before Congress. Secretary of Defense Robert Gates also testified on that day about the next steps that the military would take in repealing the policy.

Mullen, whose distinguished military career began in 1968, pointed out that he had served alongside homosexuals since he first enlisted. "Everybody in the military has," he added. Under official policy, those gay service members could be discharged on the basis of their sexual orientation, regardless of their merit as personnel. The "Don't Ask, Don't Tell" (DADT) compromise of 1993, created during the Clinton administration, was intended to allow homosexuals to remain in service so long as they did not discuss their sexual orientation or engage in sexual activity. This understanding failed to prevent more than 12,000 people from being discharged, however, and remained a rallying point for gay rights activists until the policy was finally repealed.

Don't Ask, Don't Tell

> "Mr. Chairman, speaking for myself and myself only, it is my personal belief that allowing gays and lesbians to serve openly would be the right thing to do. No matter how I look at this issue, I cannot escape being troubled by the fact that we have in place a policy which forces young men and women to lie about who they are in order to defend their fellow citizens. For me personally, it comes down to integrity—theirs as individuals and ours as an institution."

Dan Choi, a gay activist dismissed from his position in the Army because of the DADT policy, is shown here at a rally for gay rights in May 2009.

In April 2010, as President Obama visited Los Angeles for a fundraiser, his motorcade passed protesters urging him to meet his campaign promise to end the DADT policy.

President Barack Obama signed the Don't Ask, Don't Tell Repeal Act of 2010 on December 22, 2010.

> "I've talked to several of my counterparts in countries whose militaries allow gays and lesbians to serve openly. And there has been, as they have told me, no impact on military effectiveness."

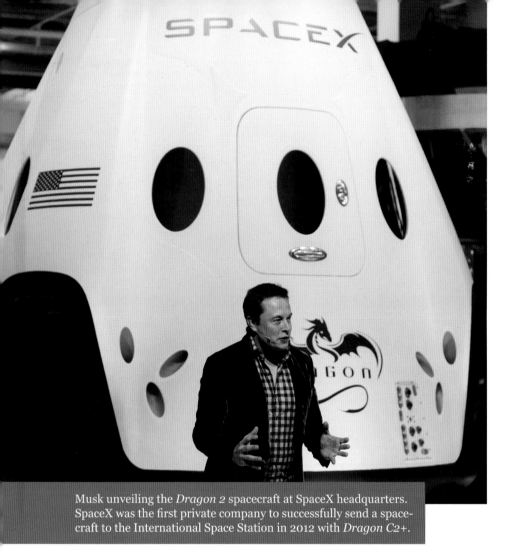

Musk unveiling the *Dragon 2* spacecraft at SpaceX headquarters. SpaceX was the first private company to successfully send a spacecraft to the International Space Station in 2012 with *Dragon C2+*.

ELON MUSK

September 28, 2017

Elon Musk, founder and CEO of SpaceX, presented an updated plan to colonize Mars at the 2017 International Astronautical Congress in Adelaide, Australia. Musk told the audience that he hoped to start building a 35-story space vehicle in 2018, launch the first rocket to Mars in 2022, and use it to land crewed missions on Mars in 2024. Musk's speech detailed plans for the Big Falcon Rocket (BFR), which could transport 100 passengers on a months-long trip to Mars, refueling several times in orbit. After landing on Mars, the BFR would be refueled using local resources before returning to Earth. The reusability of the launch vehicle and spacecraft system would make colonizing Mars economically feasible, Musk said.

Colonizing Mars

> " I think fundamentally the future is vastly more exciting and interesting if we're a space-faring civilization and a multi-planet species than if we're not. "

> " In a Mars-transit configuration, you'd essentially be taking three months in a really good scenario, but maybe as much as six months... you'd probably want a cabin, and not just a seat. "

> " In 2024 we want to try to fly four ships, two of which would be crewed... The goal of these initial missions is to find the best source of water... For the second mission, the goal is to build the propellant plant... Then build up the base, starting with one ship, then multiple ships, then start building up the city, then making the city bigger. "